WAKEFIELD PRESS

PASSION PLAY

Valerie Volk is a former secondary teacher, tertiary lecturer, and director of an international education program. She has won awards for poetry and short fiction and has published widely in journals, anthologies and magazines. Her first book, *In Due Season*, won the Omega Writers CALEB Poetry Prize in 2010, and there have been enthusiastic reviews of both her verse novel, *A Promise of Peaches*, and her sardonic modern versions of Grimms' Tales, *Even Grimmer Tales*. This fourth book, *Passion Play: The Oberammergau Tales*, reflects both a love of Chaucer's *Canterbury Tales* that was born during a Year 12 English course many decades ago and also her fascination with the infinite variety of human beings.

PASSION PLAY

THE OBERAMMERGAU TALES

Valerie Volk

Wakefield
Press

Wakefield Press
16 Rose Street
Mile End
South Australia 5031
wakefieldpress.com.au

First published 2013
Reprinted 2014
This edition published 2018

All illustrations used under licence from Shutterstock.com,
and adapted by Liz Nicholson, designBITE. Illustrations of silhouettes
of heads used on various pages, copyright 'nemiaza' and 'KatarinaF';
illustration of wavey lines used on various pages, copyright 'anfisa
focusova'; illustration of bus used on various pages, copyright
'bokononist'; illustration of girl with microphone used on various pages,
copyright 'Olemac'.

Cover designed by Leszek Hermanowicz
Text designed by Liz Nicholson, designBITE
Typeset by Wakefield Press

National Library of Australia Cataloguing-in-Publication entry

Author: Volk, Valerie, author.
Title: Passion play: the Oberammergau tales /
                Valerie Volk.
ISBN: 978 1 74305 573 1 (paperback).
Dewey Number: A823.4

CORIOLE
McLAREN VALE

Wakefield Press thanks
Coriole Vineyards for
continued support

Australian Government

Australia Council
for the Arts

Publication of this book was assisted by
the Commonwealth Government through the
Australia Council, its arts funding and advisory body.

For

Nicholas
Felicity
Samantha
Genevieve

*who have enriched my life, and shared the Oberammergau
experience, both as travellers and in other ways.*

Contents

Introduction   1

Introduction   1

The Travellers   2

Prologue: Oberammergau 1633   5

Beforehand: Sydney 2010

Caroline – her apartment   14

DAY 1   **Gathering: Munich hotel**

Caroline – the evening reception   26

Douglas: *The Knight's Tale*   33

Luke: *The Squire's Tale*   46

Francis: *The Franklin's Tale*   55

Elinor: *The Prioress's Tale*   68

DAY 2   **Travelling: Munich – Oberammergau**

Caroline – morning   92

Stephen: *The Scholar's Tale*   93

Alicia: *The Wife of Bath's Tale*   111

Bill: *The Guildsman's Tale*   132

Geoffrey: *The Doctor's Tale*   139

Alexander: *The Merchant's Tale*   153

Jethro: *The Pardoner's Tale*   168

Tommo: *The Yeoman's Tale*   184

Josef: *The Plowman's Tale*   200

DAY 3 The Passion Play: Oberammergau

Caroline – breakfast		214
Linda:	*The Cook's Tale*	216
Jack:	*The Summoner's Tale*	230
Nathan:	*The Shipman's Tale*	236
Al:	*The Miller's Tale*	253
Justin:	*The Monk's Tale*	260
Martine:	*The Manciple's Tale*	270
Tom:	*The Man of Lawe's Tale*	281
Adam:	*The Parson's Tale*	291

DAY 4 and 5 Afterwards: Oberammergau – Munich – Singapore

Caroline – return to Munich	308
Caroline – Changi Airport	322

Acknowledgements

Acknowledgements	327

Introduction

Oberammergau, a small town in the German southern Alps, is a storybook village of painted houses ornamented with Biblical and fairytale pictures, famous for the way the events of Easter week are staged each tenth year. Its Passion Play draws hundreds of thousands of people from all over the world to an event begun almost four centuries ago. Since 1634! A long time to keep this tradition, this fulfilment of a post-plague vow, alive.

Years of teaching Chaucer's fourteenth-century *Canterbury Tales* led me to realise that today's crowds who travel to the Oberammergau Passion Play are following in a long tradition, inspired by a mix of curiosity, religious faith, tourist appeal and questioning. Pilgrimages can involve many different motivations – and equally, many different outcomes.

Contemporary travellers journey from Munich to this small German town, where more than half the 5000 inhabitants are actively involved in the May – October season of full-day performances. Most modern visitors take part in a four day bus tour, a striking parallel to Chaucer's medieval pilgrimage and similar in its bringing together a group of strangers, each with his or her own story.

Chaucer's people show us a tapestry of the medieval world; my characters reveal a parallel spectrum of today's social lives. Chaucer's told fictional stories to entertain each other as they travelled. Mine also have stories, but these are their own personal tales which emerge along the way, occasionally in conversation but more often in their private thoughts. They too, like medieval pilgrims, are seeking something, whether they realise it or not, for each is caught in a web of guilt, sometimes trivial, sometimes deep-seated.

Not all find what they are looking for, or need. But then, that would be an unrealistic outcome.

Valerie Volk

The Travellers

Caroline, a newspaper features writer	*(The narrator)*
Douglas, a Cabinet Minister	*(The Knight's Tale)*
Luke, his son	*(The Squire's Tale)*
Francis, a wine merchant	*(The Franklin's Tale)*
Elinor, a school principal	*(The Prioress's Tale)*
Stephen, a research scientist	*(The Scholar's Tale)*

Alicia, a much-married socialite	*(The Wife of Bath's Tale)*
Bill, a foundry works manager	*(The Guildsman's Tale)*
Geoffrey, a gynaecologist	*(The Doctor's Tale)*
Alexander, a company director	*(The Merchant's Tale)*
Jethro, a TV evangelist	*(The Pardoner's Tale)*
Tommo, a Vietnam veteran	*(The Yeoman's Tale)*
Josef, a farmer	*(The Plowman's Tale)*
Linda, a cooking contest winner	*(The Cook's Tale)*
Jack, a schoolmaster	*(The Summoner's Tale)*

Nathan, a former pilot   (*The Shipman's Tale*)
Al, a professional footballer   (*The Miller's Tale*)
Justin, a church leader   (*The Monk's Tale*)
Martine, a businesswoman   (*The Manciple's Tale*)
Tom, a criminal barrister   (*The Man of Lawe's Tale*)
Adam, a parish priest   (*The Parson's Tale*)

and others in the tour group, including Karen, Douglas's wife, Svetla, Alexander's cousin, Mick, Blue, Paddy and Len, the foundry officials with Bill, John, an actor, Irmgard, the guide, and Friedrich, the bus driver.

Prologue

OBERAMMERGAU

1633

OBERAMMERGAU, 1633

I wait your judgement, Father.
I swear that this was not what I intended.
I swear I did not know.
You are a priest;
you know my heart.
God knows my heart.

Yet now, in search of absolution,
I must confess what I have done.
I hide here in the house in fear,
such fear, for when it is discovered,
when they find me here,
the punishment will be both swift
and terrible.

My wife, for all her seeming welcome,
now turns from me,
and will not look upon my face.
And yet it was for her that I returned.
She needed me.

Perhaps.

How could I stay there, separate,
unable to return through all those months,
while still aware that she was here alone —
and so was he …

I had departed, Father, with such doubt.
But still I had to trust, depend on her assurance
she would stay true to me.
There was such conflict in me.
I wanted to believe, to trust,
but knowing that she had betrayed before,
our parting was o'ershadowed.

A worm of fear, so stealthy,
curled itself, insidious snake,
and gnawed its way
into my very soul.

The same snake that I carved beneath the cross
there in the church where they had lured me
with their plans – an altar piece
that would adorn their fine new building –
honour more, I knew, to men than God.

Who better to carve such a special piece
than Kaspar Schisler,
known through all the valley for his work?

And then the fee!
promise of a fee that would have bought
a fine new dress for Magdalena,
and money for the winter still to come.
I thought of what it might buy for the boy.

The boy ...

He lies beneath us in the lower room.
He tosses on the bed with fever.
He cries with pain when touched.
He wears those carriers of death,
the lumps that tell us that the plague
is in our house. And in our son.
They presage what will come.
The boy ...

She wept with anguish when she saw him.
She knew, she also knew, what now would be.
And so she turns away
and will not let me near him.
Too late for that.

I braved the mountain heights to come to them.
So many months apart. With passing of each day,
I grew more certain that she would betray me.
So long without a man, and always
Karl, my brother Karl, near by,
attentive to her needs, the small gifts offered –
no matter what I said.

'But brother, Magdalena is your wife.
'Tis not unseemly that I make some small things for her
in our workshop. So if a carving's made, a small toy
for the lad, and if another trinket for your wife
is added to it, there's no harm in this.'

But brother, I have seen the way you look at her.

I wonder only now, when I recall the offer
that they made, to lure me
to the journey through the valley
to do the carving for their fine new church,
why I did not insist you went, my brother,
in my place.

But then there was my pride,
to be so asked, and with the lure of fees
like none I could earn here, bigger than
a place like Oberammergau had ever offered –
temptation that no craftsman could resist.

She, so eager for my going,
behind the guise of misery,
the pleas I might return at each week's end,
the seeming sense of loss.
I sensed what lay beneath.
But yet, I took the chance, and went.

For how could one foresee how fast the Death would spread?

How soon I'd find myself
surrounded by the stench of dying,
corpses in the streets, the shuttered houses
with their wreaths of herbs, such vain precaution
in the face of such a fiend.
I should have left the place at once,
but still I lingered, anxious to complete my work,
and earn the fee. Until too late.

They brought the news that now the road to home
was closed, that Oberammergau had made itself
a place forbidden to the outside world, with bands
of strong armed men who watched the entry routes
and turned back travellers.
Determined, all those upright citizens,
that Death would not find ways to slip by them
and so endanger those within.

I tried but once,
and they refused me entry.
Neighbours I had known since childhood
drove me back —
with anger, not with pity —
anger that I might consider bringing plague to them.

There is a limit to a man's endurance, Father.

Do not turn from me, the way that Magdalena has.
Oh yes, she took me in her arms, that first night back —
she and the boy gave me a princely welcome.
She knew what I had risked in that night journey
over mountains.

I chose my time with care.

It was the night of celebration,
the fair to honour dedication of our village church
so many years ago. The thought of Magdalena there,

perchance with Karl,
a thought that gnawed at me till unendurable.
A night when guards would be less cautious,
my chance of undiscovered entry greater.

Oh yes, I had planned well.
And I was healthy still. The plague had passed me by.
Where could there be a danger now?

I did not know what I was doing.
Where is the sin in that?

You turn away. I understand.

How many have you buried to this day?
Or in this place also, as elsewhere,
are deaths so many that the rotting bodies
are thrown in hasty pits, and covered speedily –
futile attempt to limit spread of the disease?

Now desperate, I wait in need of absolution, Father.
Already I have felt God's punishment.
The boy.
He's dearer to me than my very life.
He lies below, and she is with him.
Their deaths are on my hands.

But it was not my fault.

A man of God like you should be prepared
to hear my prayer.
You must not see me damned to hell
for now I beg for absolution.

What more now do you want?

You shake your head, and so I comprehend.
I see without this there can be no mercy for me.

I must accept the truth, the truth I have denied.
I knew full well what I was doing
when I came back.
It was my choice to come.

The guilt is mine.

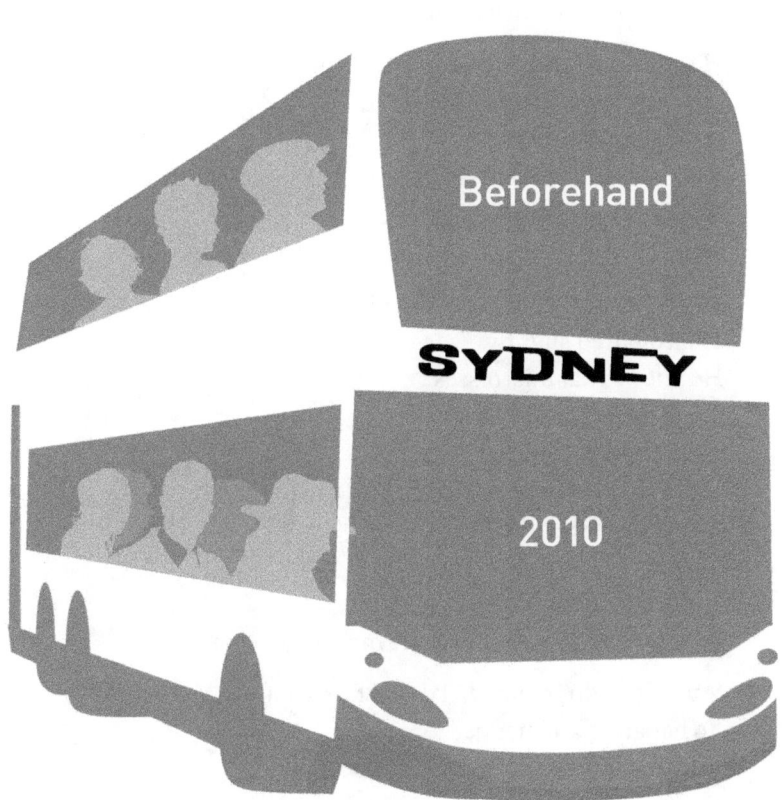

Beforehand

SYDNEY

2010

Caroline – her apartment

'But Rob,' my words that night
when he first put it to me,
'I really don't think
there will be a story in this.'

He looked at me, and settled his arm
comfortably round my shoulder,
twined his leg in mine.
I saw him glance across
to where the bedside clock
was ticking through our hour.

He sensed that I had seen the glance,
and coloured slightly.
He knows that mistresses
are sensitive to limitations on their time!
I'd warned him once
that I could bear him leaving me,
returning to her bed –
but only if he had the tact
to mask imperatives of time,
to blur the obligations of the marriage bond.

'And if you do go home,' I'd told him coolly,
'to her arms and her bed,
at least show me enough consideration
to pretend it isn't so.'
So, tacitly, we have agreed she is not there –
he tries to hide his wish to check the time.

'OK,' I said to him,
'What makes you think
there's good potential in this?'

He has a sense for where there is a tale
worth telling, a story that will interest readers,
keep circulation up, and earn smiles from the Board.
But this? I had my doubts.

And even worse, my private question.
This trip away ... device perhaps
for sending me elsewhere?
A gradual removal from his life?
Was it just possible that this would be
my exit line? Skilful manoeuvre
to separate himself from me?
(He's good at ending things,
especially his relationships.)

So by the time of my return,
it would be simple to manipulate
graceful farewells?

He has the power, that's true,
for in this mini-world that we inhabit,
editors can call the shots ...

There's more to it than this.
I may have slept with him at first
because it seemed prudential, yes.
But then I hadn't thought
that he would wind his way into my heart.
By now I feared to lose him.

'Oberammergau,' he ruminated.
'What do you know about it?'

I shook my head. 'Not much.
A passion play, whatever that might be.
Somewhere in Germany?'

'For someone who's supposed to be
an educated woman,
you have surprising gaps!'

'So tell me,' I invited,
and settled down against his shoulder.
'And why you think that there's a story here!'

It turned into a mini history lesson,
but for a time alarm clocks were forgotten.
He took me back six hundred years,
and brought the past to life.

'The sixteenth century ...' – meditatively –
'a time of death, disease, wars, famines, plague ...
You really wouldn't call it easy living.'

I hear again his voice, and nod as I did then.

So he continues to recount, some parts familiar
from my days of European history,
struggles of the time.
Wars, like the Thirty Years.

That one I know,
with all its repercussions, the religious strife,
political manoeuvres, waste of human life
(strange, how we never learn from lessons of the
    past).

But what I had not known was
how it spread the plague, how Swedish armies,
rampaging through Germany,
brought with them more than warfare's death –
they brought the dread disease that future centuries
would spread through decimated lands.

And still we think our age has brought
inventions like the global village.

How we do presume!

I lose his thread, but caught in contemplation
of this past, he hasn't noticed.

For now he's telling me of later plagues,
the nightmare world of wiped out villages
and families destroyed. He quotes the symptoms –
sickening, these, to listen to.

To suffer them would be to live, to die,
within a world of horror.
Swollen bodies.
Rotting flesh,
the blackened blisters,
blood-seeping pustules,
suffocation of the lungs,
foreseeing only certain ugly death.

Worse still, the likelihood
that all those close to you
would suffer the same fate,
infected by you.
A hideous inevitable outcome.

'Why are you telling me all this?'
I ask, with some distaste.

'Because' his voice is patient,
'you need to understand.
This is the background you will need to know.'

I marvel at his calm assumption
that it will be relevant,
that I will meet his expectations,

carry out his wishes,
go to where he sends.
But yet I know it's true. I will.

I recognise this is my briefing
for the time to come.

I hear of little villages that trembled
as plague took hold, of how they tried
in desperation to protect themselves.

We come to Oberammergau, set in its valley,
seeking only isolation from the ravaging disease,
determined to preserve itself by absolute refusal
to let the would-be travellers in or out.

Until one night a man, one only, frantic
at the separation from his wife and child,
makes secretly his journey
through tiny obscure mountain passes
and brings with him the plague.

'Yes, yes!' I interrupt. This story is so long.
Our time together is too limited
for such a history lesson.
'I understand. So they too had the plague?'

He nods, his eyes fixed on a distant point.
I know that he is seeing bodies,
bloated, stinking,
brought outside the houses,
weeping women watching daughters,
husbands, sons, loaded on to carts,
and sent to common graves,
before they go into their homes,
to wait for the same fate.

He tells me how they gathered in the church
to pray, to promise.
This now becomes familiar;
somewhere I have read of this,
and I recall the tale.

The vows they made to God that
if he spared their village
they would offer to him, time on time,
performance of a passion play,
a presentation of Christ's suffering and death.

So this would be their act of thanks –
a tribute and reminder of deliverance.

Such faith.

'Well you may scoff,' he shrugs his shoulders.
'Myself, I find simplicity like this remarkable.
But it was still an age that tolerated
the idea of miracles. In fact, believed.
Whether the cause or not, from that day on
there were no further deaths.
I guess the plague had run its course – '

(He smiles. Settles his arm more comfortably
round my shoulders. I move a little closer.
These moments with him are so precious.)

' – a fortunate coincidence of timing – '

'They kept the vow?'

'That's how it started. First presentations
in the churchyard, a stage they built
above the graves of all those victims of the plague.
Then as the decades passed,
it grew. Too big. Beyond the church.

At last they built a playhouse –
the forerunner of what we see today.'

'It's every ten years this event occurs?'
I calculate it fast.
'It must be close to forty times by now.
They've never missed?'

I hear about the two times there was no production –
again it's war and politics, imperatives
I've learned can rule the world.

'Agreed it's interesting,' I yawn.
'But I don't see that there's a story in this.'

'Ah, then you haven't understood
the scale of this event,
or what it means to those who go.'

I raise an eyebrow, quizzical, but in spite
of cynicism I am captured by
his slow account of half a million people
who journey each ten years,
flocking from remotest parts throughout the world,
to such an obscure village,
of the many who return each decade
seeking to recapture
what they've found in this event.

He tells me how the village
spends interim years in preparation,
how more than half the residents
take part in each performance,
a huge production –
more than fifteen hundred on the stage.

I marvel at his story of the old men
who started back in childhood,
babes in arms, their mothers in the crowd;
still today they dodder, totter, limp their way
through those same scenes.

By now I'm caught.
He's drawn me well into this world,
where Judases, the season over, suicided,
no longer finding themselves able
to bear the thought of whom they've been,
where Marys in the olden days were asked
to prove virginity, and where, still now,
one must be resident of twenty years,
or born there, to take part.

But still I do not see where this is heading.
What is the plan he has for me?

He starts the explanation; it takes some time
before I am convinced. Seduced,
I see the picture through his eyes.

Why do so many people come, some once
and even more time after time,
to see this play, this passion play?
Who are they, all these travellers,
week after week, month after month?

What are their stories?
What compulsions bring them here,
to this small village in the valley
beneath its towering mountains?

'There is a series here,' so he assures me.
'Stories to be told. And you – '
(the scarcely subtle smooth talk starts)

'you are the one to tell them. You have skills'
(the flattery is heavy now)
'you have the skills with people,
human sympathy that draws them out.

Just go,' he urges me. 'Just go there.
Be a part of it. They go in groups.
Join such a group, and see what you can learn.
There'll be a market for what you may discover.
And then who knows?'
(This is the bribe, the ultimate that he can offer)
'It's possible that it could make a book for you ...'
The final lure for any journalist.
So how could I refuse?

Already I am speculating. Each ten years
so many waiting eagerly to travel
to somewhere small, remote, inconsequential.
Almost – unbidden comes the thought –
almost a pilgrimage.
And that word clinches it;
the bait's been dangled.
I know that I will do this thing.
The lure of finding just why a half a million pilgrims
set forth each decade's end
is not one that I can resist.

'It's almost medieval,' I point out.

He laughs at my naiveté. 'I think we've moved
beyond their theocentric world. I doubt
there'll be too many there for reasons
that you'd call religious.
Though come to think of it, I'm not too sure
that many back in olden days were fired
by heavenly motives.

Take Chaucer's lot! You'd have to say
that they were really quite a motley crew!

But you deserve a holiday –
consider this a treat, a small reward for all your . . .
overtime.'

It's now I know that what I feared is real.
My time with him is up – the tactful exit
I'd anticipated's come.

I can at least accept with dignity
that my days in Rob's sun
have run their course. There'll be no fuss.

He's never lied – I think he's never lied to me.

Throughout, no subterfuge. No promises.
It's been quite clear his marriage and his home,
those children's faces smiling on his desk,
that these come first. The time with me
has been diversion; this too I have accepted.

I'd told myself that it was all I wanted.
A casual affair, a useful man. Attractive, too.
Until I found that somehow he had passed
through my defences, and found a place
in that untenanted abode, my heart.

So now I fear, and fear too much to voice
the questions I would like to ask.
This way there is a chance that
when I do come back
he may still laugh away my doubts,
and welcome me
into his waiting arms again.

DAY 1

GATHERING

Munich hotel

Caroline – the evening reception

'A motley crew ...' The words return.
I find them true as I survey the room.
Frenetic chat from thirty people rises
above the sounds of music.

Who,
I wonder briefly, was responsible
for choice of lilting Strauss, the waltzes
that now counterpoint strained tones
of people whose companionship
is not of their own choosing
but for a common cause?

The tour group gathers.
I note the way our hostess
makes determined efforts to create
a truly 'happy hour.' Her eyes are
sheepdogs, gathering together strays
who haven't joined the flock.

With practised ease she notes a single man,
who clearly seeks to stay detached,
and shepherds him
to where I stand alone.

Her introductions show she's done her homework;
the cheat sheet that she carries
is scarcely needed as she murmurs that
we will have things in common: he,
an actor, is clearly destined for this
travel writer, for so I have portrayed
myself. The truth, as always, is a tad
manoeuvrable.

'The Arts, you know ...' she murmurs,
and departs.

We stand, apparently at ease, but
secretly already counting hours until
these carefully arranged proximities
can cease. We talk about his work,
his interest in this play as theatre,
the masses it draws in. 'Amazing,'
we concur. 'And for such centuries!'

The casual social niceties explored,
I question whether he knows
others in the room. So we begin
to survey, speculate, assess our
fellow-travellers. The range is
language-simplified; this is an English
speaking group. Relief – this makes my task
a little easier, I swiftly realise.

The man beside me beckons to
a passing waiter, gets us refills,
(a second-rate champagne, we have agreed)
and then, corralled but uncomplaining,
accepts his situation and tells me
what he's learned this afternoon.
A filling in of time since his arrival
before tonight's enforced conviviality.
Impressive – just how much he's found!
'A useful coffee with our tour guide,' he explains.

John points to figures I might know.
A politician ... yes, I too have read
the pundits' comments he's in danger
and will likely lose his seat.

Some scandal from his life, uncovered
by too zealous a young man. I don't feel
any need to make admissions that it was
my paper which released that story.
Better not to be associated with the gutter press.

Another face I've seen in print too often –
a socialite who's graced our pages many times –
that polished smile is one I know so well.

'And with her,' he informs, 'prospective spouse
material. Gossip says he's fated to be
husband number five … I'd have to say
he looks quite comfortable in the role.
Must be the reason that she's here. A tour
like this is really not her scene at all.'

'And are there others here you've met?'

He tells me of the television chef – who won
a cooking contest; her prize money
is paying for this travel. Then, next to her,
another face familiar on the box, especially
Sunday mornings, when TV evangelicals
provide a road to heaven for the gullible.

'I'm pretty sure this trip is an investment.'

I like his cynicism. The quick acerbic summaries
are useful fodder for my task. Standing,
glass in hand, we still survey the room.

A little cluster by the makeshift bar.
Good old boys, all – a reminiscent phrase,
that takes me back to southern gentlemen
on jazz-filled nights in New Orleans, red-faced
and paunchy, mourning still the loss

of white supremacy. Good old boys
wanting back the good old days. But these
are different. They're Aussie mates, enjoying
to the full their German beer.

I raise an eyebrow, interrogative.
My new-found friend obligingly fills in
the details. A last stage, this,
a side trip for the chaps,
fresh from their tour fact-finding,
checking out the changes in production
that will be the base for competition
from their counterparts abroad.

'Not sure what field,' reluctantly admitted.
(He's proud of his prowess, enjoys the gossip.
I speculate, surmise he's gay.)
'I think it's possibly a foundry where they work.'

It's clear that their research time's over;
I wonder only why they're on this tour,
for Oberammergau is not a likely choice.
Perhaps some travel agent, pursuing an agenda
not entirely suited to her clientele.
Fish out of water, I decide.

But they are not the only ones.
A lad stands, petulant and bored,
his Mohawk hair a clear aggressive challenge
to preconceptions of his elders.
Though closer scrutiny will soon confirm
he's not the youth I'd thought.
He's in his twenties, far more likely,
but assuming such a look of teenage angst
that he could well be locked

into a decade earlier. 'Politician's son,'
is murmured by the figure at my side.
'I somehow don't think
that he volunteered to join our pilgrimage . . .'

I glance up sharply at him. I am surprised
to hear the word that I have thought my own
articulated by this man.

'Oh yes,' he echoes my unspoken thought.
'We're really quite a crew. That little group
the agent's chatting up – she clearly knows
the ones who are important. The man beside her – '

'With the monocle?' I interrupt.
It's something that one doesn't often see.

' – very well-known. Top man in his field.'

'Which is?'

'A gynaecologist. My wife assured me
he was excellent. My ex-wife, actually.
Number three.'

'Well, well,' I murmur lightly. 'Always good
to know a man as skilled as that.
And is there number four?'

'I really feel that after three I've learned a lesson.
Wouldn't you?' He glances at my ringless fingers;

I answer the unspoken question. 'Not any more.'

We look again at others in that group.
No one I recognise. But my companion does.
The churchman on the right, I learn,
is well in line to be the next Archbishop –
'especially,' comes another comment,

somewhat barbed, 'once he's acquired
a freshened odour of the sanctity
that Oberammergau might give . . .'

'Or maybe,' he continues, musing further,
'that's why Tom Gillooley's here. You know,
of course, just who he is?'

'The name's familiar, but I can't quite think.'

'Defended in that fraud case,
the one where half the top men walked away,
and mum and dad investors lost their shirts.'

By now, I see potential in this group.
For, as I glance around the room, I note
the little knots of those determined
to be sociable. I see they're interspersed
by singles who, like me,
try to maintain a poise,
refusing to be daunted by their solitude.

Gathered here, we're waifs and strays,
like Chaucer's pilgrims on their trek
to Canterbury.
Is Munich giving us another Tabard Inn?
But there will be no saint's tomb at the end
of this, our pilgrimage.
Oh yes, I've done my homework pre-departure.
I've learned about those people as they gathered
six hundred years or more ago.

I wonder how they felt as they surveyed
their fellow travellers on the road.

I can see here what Robert has already sensed.
I hear again his question. Why are they here?

These thirty people – eager, apprehensive, bored,
    unwilling –
these people have their stories.
Whether I can learn them –
that's not so sure. If it were possible
to get inside their minds, to hear their thoughts,
the memories, dreams, the wishes, unfulfilled desires
that bring them to this place. Ah, then
I'd have the stories that I need.

So where would I begin?

I scrutinise the room again and see
a likely starter, on his own. The man
whose story all our readers found quite titillating.

The newsroom had been tipping that
his life in politics would be rewarded
in next year's Honours List:
another MP finds himself a knight?

Doubtful now.

He stands there, solitary; looks across the room
to where his wife is centre of a knot of men.
She glances at him, looks away unsmilingly.
Her hero knight? But yes, what feet of clay.

There's precedent to call on: so

'and at a knight than wol I first biginne ...'

DOUGLAS: THE KNIGHT'S TALE

He never yet no vileinye ne sayde
In al his lyf, unto no maner wight.
He was a verray parfit gentil knight.

༄

He never yet a boorish thing had said
In all his life to any, come what might,
He was a true, a perfect gentle-knight.

I dreamed last night about her.
She doesn't haunt me –
but I find I cannot meet her eyes.

The boy has the same eyes.
In every other way he looks like me.
It's no surprise that everyone believed the story
the moment that they saw those pictures
that daily papers ran with such indecent gusto.

I watch the lad across the room.
He's restless, not at ease.
Dark hair on end – one day she asked me:
'How does he keep it up like that?'
My wife's tone was aloof and disapproving.
I know she yearns to slick it down.
In honesty, I do myself!

But she is cautious what she says to him –
or to me. We circle warily, like lions,
knowing somewhere
there is prey, a carcass waiting for us,
but hesitant to make the pounce.
A pounce might tear this fragile skin
that we have carefully constructed.

Not skin. We walk on ice, perilous,
afraid, and conscious always
of depths that stir with restless expectation
of time when we will fracture devastatingly
so thin a film across the deep.

I feel the shrug with which he turns to look at me.
There is a bond between us that we can't deny.
He's flesh of mine, and blood.

I read his thoughts, his mood, with an uncanny ease.
Not that he seeks to hide his boredom,
clear distaste with which he views the gathered crowd.

It still surprises me – the readiness with which
(casual lift of shoulders, true)
he said that he would come.
He couldn't have expected feeling easy
in such a group as this. We're older, staid,
our interests certainly not his.

One occasion I did hear his band.
Totally dismayed, at last aware
of just how out of touch I am
with everything his generation values.

A dark and smoky pub, entry stamp
upon my hand, raucous noise
of all the early groups. Long intervals,
while tangled labyrinths of cords and wires
were carefully dismantled. Garish instruments
carried reverentially from tiny stages.
Next groups waiting with impatience
for moments in the spotlight.

'We'll be on late,' he'd warned me.

Perhaps his tacit 'Don't you come!'

But always somewhere in me a real need
to share his life, on any sort of basis.
I'd steeled myself, so many years ago,
to play my role: godfather! Well, in subtle ways,
I was. For Fran had been quite adamant.

'I don't want him to know. It's risky for you.
If he thinks you were just his father's friend,
a kindly uncle type, it's safer for us all.'

That's very well, but surely he himself
has sometimes noticed the resemblance,
and had to keep subduing thoughts
or awkward questions?

Most probably his mother found some answers.
She's good at that.
And so determined they would not intrude
into my other life.

'I'll take the money, yes.
That's only fair, that you should be responsible.
He is your son. I won't have him deprived.
But here's the deal. He'll think that Daryl
was his dad. And so he might have been,
if he'd been shipped home in his uniform
instead of in a coffin. Or if he'd slept with me
those nights of his last leave.

No Doug, you didn't take advantage
of my grief. I knew what I was doing
the day you came to bring his things.

I'd never claim I went into it blindly;
I sensed that all the time your feelings
were more complex than you knew.
A sort of horror, even –

maybe you felt you occupied a dead man's shoes.
Or bed, perhaps?'

Today, though more than twenty years have passed,
I shudder at the memory of her words.
Too true. How well she knew me, way back then.
She knew that all my life was planned,
and circumscribed. My job, my goals, ambitions –
Karen sharing everything,
the decades of our marriage.

Never any thought of leaving her.

Fran did not expect it. Even want it,
I thought, self-righteous young cub that I was.
No, no excuse in that. At thirty eight, I knew
what I was doing. But Fran was generous.
She knew how much I loved the child,
my yearning for a son.

'As long,' she pointed out, 'as long as we live
in another state, it's possible for you to be with us.
A loving godfather, who comes to visit,
a father figure for his best friend's son.'

An irony, indeed. Yet it sufficed.

Fortunate to be in a position where long absences
from home were quite acceptable,
and where extended stays
and stretches interstate did not bring questions.

A double life? That's what the papers called it.
But still I do not know just how disclosure came.

Not Fran, I'm sure. Her care for me, my reputation,
was absolute. Her certainty that Karen must not know.

'For that,' she said, 'would be unbearable for her.
To know that someone else had given you a son,
when she could not.'

It matched with her dismayed response,
when first she told me of her pregnancy.
I asked, repugnant as it was, her plans.
I wondered whether she intended on her own
to have the child.

Her face closed coldly, and she said,
'It's all I'll ever have of you. And all I'll ask.'

She kept her bargain well. There were no needs
and no demands expressed. A home provided
when I could be with them. A role in my son's life,
although he did not know it.

The irony! The day he said to me:
'I sometimes wish I'd got to know my dad,
but Uncle Doug, you've been just like a dad
to me.'

So hard, to swallow back the words
that clogged my throat.

Like me, he looks around the room.

We stand, a wary group,
some desperate for friendship
in touching eagerness to find rapport,
others assuming casual poise,
attempting with an equal desperation,
to look convincingly detached.

It's these who make the tour guide's job
a nightmare; to weld this disparate crew
into some semblance of togetherness.

Four days of bonhomie – no matter if it's fake,
as long as they return with smiling faces
and shared email addresses,
she will feel success.

I don't foresee her chances of success with Luke as great.

Why has he come? I'm still not even sure
why we have asked him. Karen's idea.
'I need to know him. He's your son. The child
I could not give you. He's all we'll ever have.
I need to share him with you.'

Impossible indeed to deny her. I owe too much.
The costs of reparation will be high.
This trip a small drop in a bucket
it will take me years to fill.

I turn to look towards her. She stands,
as always, elegant. Composed, her face still lovely,
even now, as age begins to take its toll.
Not only age. The public scrutiny
that she has undergone these last few months
has left its mark –
her mouth compressed a little more, a line
between her brows that's new,
her smile more brittle than it used to be.

I watched her deal, in courteous dismissal,
with newsmen snapping at her heels,
and brush past TV cameras, relegating them
to other worlds in which she had no place.

I felt my heart swell with the old
familiar love and pride.
Then in the quiet of the house,
she kept the same cool poise.

No tears and no recriminations,
just two questions:
How? And why?

The first, a simple answer. She deserved the truth.
The second: quite impossible to find the words
to make it clear to me, as much as to my wife,
why I had done this to us.

Will you resign?
They caught me at the airport,
asking the same question:
'Minister, will you contest the seat again?'

They are like hounds that, scenting blood,
cannot be drawn away. A two day wonder!
'What did the PM say?
Your resignation? Is that what he wants?'

'I'm not concerned,' he'd said. At first.

'Let's face it, Douglas, you are not the only one
to have a little extra in your life.
The days when revelation of a child born out of wedlock –
now, there's a mid-Victorian idea for you! –
could shock the voters are well and truly over.
How many years have we been friends?
I'm not about to sack you from the ministry
because a bit of revelation of your private life
has got into the press!'

But pressures as the days went by –
talk-back shows and women's magazines
took up the cudgels on behalf of all mistreated women,
and lurid tales of double lives erupted –
till even he, old friend or not, began to doubt
the wisdom of my staying on.

A great capacity he has to weigh up damage,
then assess to what extent
I now might be a liability.

Ironic, this, indeed. A life in which the Party
always has been my first thought.
A life devoted to the people that I stood for –
who will remember this?

The moment scandal hits, all else goes by the board.

I look back down the years: so many battles fought,
so much else sacrificed, and always for the common good.
I dare assert those words because, right from the start,
I have believed in this.

It goes down deep;
it comes from way way back. An idea
I would never think to share with others.
Days of idealism. Youth. My own.
I see myself, a young man, eager and naïve,
intently listening
as an older man, philosopher, shares visions.
I see us reading wisdom of the past,
ideas implanted early, even in the murky world of politics.

In Plato's ideal state, he asks in his *Republic*,
who are the shepherds who will guide
and guard their world?

So deeply this young man internalises the idea
that men of honour, intellect and thinkers,
these should be the rulers of the land,
these king philosophers.

It's locked away inside his psyche.
Only Karen knows how deeply
he has kept this guiding force in life and work,

this ideal of the good, with men in power
whose role should be to bring about this world.

As years have passed,
he's tried to keep the faith.
The battles he has fought have had one link —
this vision of the good.

He knows and is embarrassed by his reputation,
a Don Quixote figure, tilting sometimes
at the windmills others saw, in his mind
dragons, monsters, that needed his resistance.
While to his people, his electors, someone they
could trust, who'd fight their battles too.

So though he shrugged aside the public image,
somewhere deep down he knew he took
a little shameful pride in it. It hurts, to see it go.

It hurts still more to see that those who sneered
(he's always known it) at his steadfast refusal
to pad accounts, to take the perks that came his way,
to stick to letter of the law, are watching now
with smirks and covert sniggers his decline,
his fall from grace. Another poppy cut right down,
and laughter at the sly dog in their midst.

Who'd ever credit it? Old Dougie, eh?
A woman in another state for twenty years.
A bastard kid! Just goes to show how all that uprightness
was just a sham. He winces at the thought.
It has corroded more than just the public image.
It has destroyed his picture of himself.

The man I was, he thinks, he's gone for ever.

But Karen's still here with me;
I marvel at this thought.

She's working this room, as she's always worked
the countless cocktail parties, opening nights, suppers
in small halls at local party meetings. She's charming
this assorted crew, just as she's charmed
the countless party secretaries and difficult officials,
as much at ease with young mums
as with the blue rinse ladies of fund-raising groups.

Though only I, of this I'm sure, have seen
the desperate yearning on her face, as she's bent
    over prams,
and cooed at countless infants down the years.
Unfair! Unfair! That she, so anxious for a child,
should be denied. Her prayers, unanswered
by her god, but yet she kept her faith.

All she's asked of me is that, each tenth year,
we should make this trip.
Each time we join a group like this;
for her it is important.
She sees it as renewal of her faith, consolidation.

I come. I watch. I wonder. Her certainty is moving,
even while I am bewildered by it.
I see this play as spectacle,
a good man, treated so unjustly.
It fills me once again
with passion to continue that same struggle that he knew –
a fight to bring about a better world.

To come this year, though. Surely a mistake?
It smacks of running from the hounds.
But not to come would be a deep betrayal
of all that we have shared.
For God himself, if he existed,
would know that I have hurt,
betrayed too much already, this woman whom I love.

There's little that I could deny her now,
but still I doubt the wisdom
of her wish to bring the boy.
I cannot gauge just what it is she wants.
I see her looking at him, with intensity.
She studies him – it's almost like a scientist
and he the bug beneath her microscope.
Is he aware of how she scrutinises him?
How does he feel?

It was his choice to come.

I made the offer diffidently,
with no belief that he'd accept.
It's strange and sad, almost as if those twenty years
of easy friendship with him, affection that we shared,
are suddenly wiped out.
His eyes are cold and unforgiving, for now
the bond we've had is broken by a knowledge
I almost wish he had not gained.

I wonder if his mother always planned
that final revelation to him.

As what? A long-delayed anticipated punishment,
retaliation for her years of relegation
to side paths in my life?

Or was it that she felt it was his birthright,
the right to know
whose son he really was?

More likely, so it seems to me,
that in that haze of her last day,
those moments when the doctors made it clear
her injuries were past repair, that there was nothing more
that they could do, perhaps in all her last confusion
truth slipped out, and so she told him.

Truth's like that – a slippery little number.
You think you have it nailed, but then it slides away,
and you are left once more, with flimsy residues
of what you thought were tablets carved in stone.

No wonder Pilate asked the question
that has haunted mankind down the years – and then
was given no answer. 'What is truth?'

Well, Fran gave Luke the truth. I wonder how she put it.

I guess I'll never know.
He steadfastly refuses to tell me about it.
Won't even talk about the accident, or how she died.

Just came to me and said it simply.
'Mum said to me before she died
that you're my father. Is it true?'

It didn't even cross my mind to cast doubt on her story,
nodded mutely, said I wished we'd told him,
years before.

There were no reconciliation scenes, no weeping
on each other's shoulder, only tacit recognition
that everything had changed.

But how much more it was to change,
I still did not foresee.

My only thought was whether to tell Karen.

That decision wasn't mine to make,
for in the end reporters did it for me.

However they discovered it … well, hardly relevant.
Too many people in that hospital, some lawyer's clerk,
who knows? My world has crashed around me.
I struggle desperately to dig a tunnel to relief.

To throw away a life in which I think I've done some good,
abandon chances to continue with the tasks ahead?
Is this the best decision?

Or stay and fight, accept opprobrium,
and learn to live with this new image,
spattered and besmirched?

I turn to Karen — always there as friend and confidante,
as wife and lover; there's comfort in her arms.

She says that she does not condemn.
She sees me still, she says, as a good man
caught in a situation that he did not plan,
and trying to do right by everyone.

But this is what she says.

I catch her looking at me;
I know she sees a stranger,
The man whose face the mirror shows me,
the man I do not know.
The bond is broken, but, without her,
is there any way I can go on?

Then there's the lad. He stares at me,
and turns away. Not hard to know
what's in his mind. Much harder
to foresee where we can go from here.

LUKE: THE SQUIRE'S TALE

With him ther was his sone, a yong Squyer...
Of twenty yeer of age he was, I gesse

He had his son with him, a fine young Squire ...
He was some twenty years of age, I guessed

Wish to God I knew
just why I've come here with them.
I have a few ideas.
They're standing over there,
the two of them. In spite of everything
they're holding it together.

God, they make me puke.
Show. Show. It's always show
with them. The perfect couple.
I guess that's not the way
that people see them now!

I used to like the old sod.
Can't believe it now.
He took me in, the way
he's taken in the whole wide world.
Guess it's the way
he took her in – my mum.

Can't bear to think
of them in bed together.
See him sticking it in her.
Wonder if she moaned.
'Oh, Dougie, Dougie,
give me more.' Wonder
if he slept with her

whenever he came over.
Sneaking down the hallway
to her room? Waiting
till I went to sleep?
Every time, perhaps?

And me, not knowing.
All excited, every time
he came there. 'Luke,
Uncle Doug is coming
next weekend.' I see me now,
a stupid little kid, thinking
of the gift that he'd bring.

'Can we go meet him at the airport?'
She'd shake her head
and tell me that he had
some business to attend to first.
After that he'd come to us.

Or wonder where he'd take me
this trip. While all the time
he's banging Mum at night.
'It was just once,' she told me
right before she died.
Lying bitch. A pretty
bloody likely tale that was.
As if she'd get a kid
from just one fuck.
Who does she think she'd fool
with such a story!

Christ, I need a hit.
It's all that keeps me going
when I stop and think
about the two of them together.
And of the way they had me

fooled for years. The lies
she told. 'He was your Dad's
best friend. That's why
he's taking care of us.'

What crap! And me, the sucker,
wet behind the ears, who
thought that Uncle Doug
was Superman and Gary Ablett
rolled in one. He'd take me out
to parks to kick a footie round.
I'd like to kick his head in now.

Wonder what my chances are
of scoring in this place.
I'm loaded now, but that'll
soon run out. Gotta find
a place to deal. Only way
I'll make it through the next
few days with them. Find a band –
there's always someone there
who's carrying. First get through
this crappy gathering. The wrinklies
and the wannabees – wankers all.

Dougie and her ladyship
fit in real well. Can't stand the way
she looks at me, especially
when she thinks that I can't see her.
Tries so fucking hard
to be my friend. Stupid cunt
just doesn't have a clue.
No idea of what I think of her.

I think of Mum and how she lived.
OK. She said she loved her work.
But then I look across the room

and see that bitch, who has
the life that should have been
my Mum's. All very well for Mum
to say it was her choice. That
it was her who told him how
she wanted it to be, that he
could come and see us when
he could. I bet it wasn't
what she really wanted.
And how that bastard could agree
to such a scheme!

Makes me sick to think
how I admired him once.
Felt really proud to say at school
he was my godfather.
What a joke! The joke's on me.
He had an image, see!
A pollie one could trust. Someone
you could rely on. There's nothing
in this life you can rely on.
Except the little pills, of course.
They give you what they promise.

What did she see in him, my Mum?
Or did he take advantage
when he came, oozing sympathy?
Telling stories of his mate, the man
I'd always thought my Dad.
A hand first on her knee, and then
around her shoulders, moving on …
Reminds me of a play we read at school.
It was a Shakespeare, I remember that.
Hamlet, I reckon. A guy who found
his mother with his uncle. Then I
didn't get it. The way he felt. Now

I do. 'A pair of reechy kisses' –
didn't know I could bring back
that line. Not even sure just what
it means – but it sounds like them.
Ugly. I blot it out in any way I can.

Only fair the money that he gives me
goes on buying what I need. No,
not 'I need.' 'I want.' I'll stop it
any time I choose to. It's not the way
I plan to spend my life, chasing
the next score from lane to lane.
Though that would show him.
Settle her hash too. I wonder
how she'd take a junkie for a son.

Trying to work out just what
she wants from me. There's something
in the way she watches me.
Quite freaky. She's after something.
He says he wants things back
the way they used to be. Dream on.
That just won't happen, Pop!

I like to keep them guessing.
Every time they think they might be
getting somewhere with me, change
my tactics, shift things round.
Dropping out of uni … easy. Never
wanted it in any case. Only really
liked the band we had there. Don't
bother with that any more. Who cares!
More fun to get high, wander round
the pubs at night, crash at a mate's.
There's always someone holding. But
I'm finding lately that the pills
don't do it for me. 'Try a bit of this,'

was Con's idea last week. A quick
crash course in how to find the vein
and in it slid. Hard to describe the bliss.
A world where suddenly it all was good.
I think that's going to be the way to go.
Another one for 'Uncle Doug' to handle.

Christ knows he had to get me out
of scrapes at school. So now I know
real well just how to push his buttons.
I think she knows that money's going
from her purse. Strange how she's started
putting it away more carefully when
I'm around. Suspicious bulge
under her pillow when I went upstairs
last week. Always a useful time
to have a look around when they're downstairs.
I reckon that their room's
fair game. Just tit for tat. I bet
my Mum's room was fair game for him.

Makes you think, though – what woman
puts her purse under her pillow!
She'd have to be a real untrusting cow!
That cost her a cool fifty. She looked
at me, but didn't say a word.

It was the day they asked me if
I'd come along with them; this trip
to Germany, a weirdo deal if ever
there was one. Some little town
and some religious stuff I'd never
heard of. But I figured that they thought
they ought to ask the long-lost son along.

They never thought I'd come. I guess
that's why I said I would. Got to

keep them on the hop. He's looking
older these days; so is she. 'We need
to get away,' she said. 'It's been
hard on your dad ...' I watch her carefully,
check to see the look I'm waiting for
whenever she says 'dad' to me. He told me
that she wasn't able to have kids. Another
bit of useful info. I can get her there.
I like to get the words 'my mum' into
our conversations. Her lips smile,
but it doesn't reach her eyes.

'It's been a tough time for him, Luke,'
she says again. 'I think he feels
his life in politics is over. And unfair!'
her voice is passionate. 'Unfair when
he has done so much. And always good.
He's tried to do the best for everyone.
Especially you.' I nod, and try to keep
my lip from curling, choke down
the words I'd like to say. Instead, 'Yeah,
it was real bad luck that it got into
all the papers. Wonder how they knew.'

She's grateful that I'm talking to her.
Doesn't know I came along exactly
for this reason. Twist the knife a little.
'He'd been so careful to avoid it
being known. I can't imagine how
it got to be a public scandal.' I shake
my head, mirror her dismay, and try
to hide the grin that rises in me.

They always told me that the contacts
one makes at university
would be worthwhile.
They're right. They did pay off.

A few words here and there
and Bob's your uncle – or
in this case 'Doug's my dad'
– and it was done.

Caroline

Tonight when I get back I'll email Rob.
Just let him know that all is going well.
I'm doing as he wanted, part of this tour group,
potential's looking good.

May tell him something of the people,
keep him in touch with what he has commissioned.

That boy I've just been watching, for example.
curious, the way he looks at mum and dad –
of course she's not his mother really –
must be a tricky situation. But why on earth
would he come here with them? With us?

Who am I fooling? Email Rob to tell him this?
Email Rob and hope I may hear back!
that's more the truth of it.

Forget this. Go and talk to someone else.

FRANCIS: THE FRANKLIN'S TALE

A Frankeleyn was in his companye ...
To liven in delyt was ever his wone,
For he was Epicurus owene sone,
That heeld opinioun, that pleyn delyt
Was verraily felicitee parfyt.

❧

A land-owner, a Franklin, had appeared ...
He lived for pleasure and had always done,
For he was Epicurus' very son.
In whose opinion sensual delight
Was the one true felicity in sight.

'But then, this isn't your first tour to Oberammergau?'
she asks, her finely-pencilled brows enquiring.

An interesting question. How does she know?
It certainly suggests that she has done research
about her fellow tourists. It makes me wonder.

Perhaps she hasn't quite absorbed the fact
that I'm once more attached;
no longer on the list of men
who just might be available. Surprising.
I would have thought her far too young,
too much to offer, to take an interest in a man my age.
But yet she seems to know a bit about me;
is it just curiosity that brings her to my side?

Not so surprising. There's a look that women get
when they are on the hunt; it's what I see
in her eyes now. I've learned to recognise it.
Six years as widower have made me wary.

Too many dinner parties where the hostess greets me,
speculative glances, an arch look:
'Oh Francis, have you met … Virginia/Alice/Cecily …?
The list goes on. I half regret I haven't kept
a widower's log book! I could at least
have published a checklist, something as a guide
for others similarly placed.

Those tortured dinner parties, with married couples
bickering within accustomed bounds of rituals
that their domestic habits have prescribed
through long years of accommodations.
How well I know it. All familiar territory.

The same paths I had walked
for more than thirty years with Pamela.
One learns a pattern of behaviour –
some things safe territory for reproaches,
sly digs, laughter in a public place;
the others – serious concerns – these we save
for times in private when the knives are out.

But yet at times they overlap.
For that's when faces become set,
and laughter has an edge of bitterness.

So Pammy, joking oh so merrily, about her lack
of time with me, about our contact mainly being
in cars, her chief role chauffeur in my life, the way
we'd never need a GPS to get us to an airport,
our car locked into automatic routing to an airfield,
its most common destination –
we all could see the steel beneath her jocularity.

Elspeth, her quips about Jim's known propensity
for secretaries who were well-endowed
in all the vital areas, would laugh

at dinner tables while we shared the joke.
Much more convenient not to notice
the excessive glitter in her eyes.

In spite of all, the comfort and familiarity
that years of pairdom had created, something
to preserve, not jeopardise. Valued.

No wonder then that willing friends were eager
to see me once again resume that life,
matching me with yet another sacrificial offering.
Question though,
which of us was to be laid upon the altar?
Or both to be stretched out, our necks prepared
and readied for the coupling yoke?
A general act of charity?

Those years of hospitality now proved themselves
an excellent investment. Invitations flowed,
and in the last six years there's rarely been
a time when I have lacked for company.

I've always known myself to be gregarious –
still another basis for complaint –
it's all too easy to recall words often spoken.
Her face, sometimes regretful, others angry,
often only resignation:
'We're always busy, never time alone.
Sometimes I think you're happiest
when we are with a crowd of others.'

Spoken lightly, in the main, but still a truth we recognised.

I was my happiest when in the company of others.
Family life was satisfying, but most of all
when children brought homes friends,
or in the gatherings of people whom we knew,
the neighbourhood events, the barbecues,

picnics on the beach,
and best to sit as head of my own dinner table,
with Pamela at the foot, and see myself,
the genial host, dispensing cheer with food and wine.
'You have a gift,' a friend said once to me, 'a gift
for hospitality.'

It was a compliment I treasured then,
and still do. It fitted well with both
my private and my public world.
A wine merchant can scarcely bypass
sampling his own wares.
Excuse too for the travel that I loved,
and chances to explore small vineyards,
France, Italy, and Germany, that brought a pleasure
needing to be decently downplayed, and masked
under the guise of necessary business.

'Oh yes,' I once heard my wife say,
in conversation with a friend, 'A great dad.
Francis is a real paterfamilias –
that is, of course, when he is here …'
Other occasions when she labelled me,
another public joke,
'the quintessential husband – genus absentee.'
Perhaps I laughed somewhat immoderately.
Beneath I felt the truth of what she said.
Yet through it all we both knew
that I loved her – in my way.
Terrific mother, excellent hostess. My wife.

These days at dinner parties eager hostesses
cast covert glances that explore the future possibilities
of partners who have been selected for me.

And equally, I fully realise,
my suitability for them: the widows,

saddened or relieved divorcees,
and those who have so far, by choice or accident,
avoided matrimonial bliss.

I've learned so well the swift surveying glance
that looks me over, either shyly tentative
'What will he think of me?'
Or the more poised and certain
'Might he do for me?'
For this is a meat market, of the not too subtle kind.

At worst, the desperate gaiety of those
who've tried too many times before.
At best, the frank complicity
of those who know the scene,
and join me in a sort of wry amusement.
If we are not the entertainment,
we must at least sing for our supper.

It is the eyes, those frank appraising eyes,
that give the signal. They may ask 'Suitable?'
(this from the ones who know that,
if they choose, they can get any man)
or else they query, if their owners are less sure
of their prowess in drawing others to them:
'Available?'

For here they want some reassuring sign
that you are looking too. This one today,
who stands here, just a bit too close,
and lifts her champagne glass
towards me, she's a Class A, so very sure of self.
She's taking care, she'll be the botox type, a shade
too carefully made up, with darkened hair streaked
most effectively, a triumph of a good hair salon.

I nod, and she continues: 'So why again?
What brings you here a second time?'
She's careful not to indicate
the possibilities, lest in her tone of voice
she might give clues to attitudes
that later on she may prefer to disavow.
I'm equally unwilling to commit myself.

'Oh, many things. It's interesting. It's a rare experience.
The way that this tradition lasts, has done so
through the centuries.
And I was here for business anyway …'

She seizes on the clue, and there begins our interchange.
My line of work? Wine-buying. She knows a bit.
Enough to talk with some degree of expertise
on changing trends in drinking, of new varieties
that have achieved a popularity in recent years.

What do I think of Tempranillo?
She has the wine talk pat, and talks of rich dark flavours
with the hints of plum and blackberries,
the rise of reds in Germany, the way in which
the Riesling of tradition is being overtaken
by new trends. I praise a wine, a pinot noir,
that I have drunk last week; she knows enough
in answering to use its proper name, and tells me
of the *Spätburgunder* that a friend bought for her
recently in Baden.

I am impressed. But glad that we have turned
the conversation far away
from her initial question. Why am I here?

Even to friends, this is the question I've not answered.
Easy to fob off people with a general comment.

It's not an issue I'd address with anyone.
Not our children, though Richard did remember
that Pamela and I had made this trip before.
He asked: 'But didn't you and Mum go there,
a long time back? It must have been ten years ago?
I think it was the year I'd finished my degree.
You almost missed my graduation.
That would have really pissed me off.
But then, you were away so much
it would have been quite usual!'

Ouch! But it was true. I never seemed to be around
for Sports Days, or for the school events
that Pammy photographed in multitudes of shots
'so that your Dad can see it too.'
She covered for me well.

However, I just nodded. Told him that we'd always
planned that we'd return another time. He shot
a quick look at me, saw I didn't want to talk
about it, turned the conversation elsewhere.
We don't talk much, but then we never have.
After the accident, he tried to find out just
how I was coping, tried to make me open up.
But ultimately saw it wasn't going to happen.
Habits of a lifetime can't be broken.

I find it easier in conversation with the girls,
but in our family we all know there are some things
that aren't up for discussion.

So even there, with Bet and Lee,
I wouldn't have been telling them
just how important those four days
in Oberammergau had been to us.
They've never known how close
we came to breaking up.

For Pam had kept her other life well-hidden,
and they would never have suspected
that their mother, dependable domestic figure,
was likely to have had another love.
Nor, to be honest, would I ever have foreseen
that night when Pamela came to me,
and told me there was someone else.
'Someone,' she said, and it was like her,
honest, forthright,
'Someone I care for very much. And he for me.
Besides,' this bit was tinged with malice,
'Besides, he's always here for me.'

It was a troubled time. Shaky, economically.
In fact, next term's school fees were looking
hard to meet. Now this, a blow beneath the belt.
I knew I'd taken her for granted.
But I also knew how much she meant to me.
What losing her would do.

I think she was surprised to find how much
I cared for her. I think that I was too. I had
a trip to Germany booked for that month –
it couldn't be put off. But yet I knew that,
if I went and left her, that would be the end.

'Come too,' I urged. 'We'll work this out.
I love you, and I cannot do without you.'

So many clichés, but all true. She said she'd come,
then added her proviso. We'd go to Oberammergau.

I hadn't heard of it back then, but anything –
anything to get us back on track. I wasn't one
for the religious stuff. She'd gone to church,
most Sundays, took the kids, but not a topic that
we talked about. It seemed to me that it was habit.

Another thing that I discovered. It was more.

I won't pretend that trip has changed my attitudes.
I've got a cautious feeling where religion sits.
Maybe it's so, but then again, who knows?
Hard to believe. A thinking man finds much of that
too hard to swallow. At school it had been different.
There the brothers drilled it into us, and for a time
I really did it all. Choir boy and acolyte as well.

A short time in the uni world and out at work, then
those days were gone. But still I'd have to say,
even to the non-believer that I was,
the Passion Play's impressive.
That's the word. It did make an impression.

For Pammy it was something more. It seemed
to help her find herself again, make up her mind.
For both of us, a time to be together, find again
what once we'd had. Or if not that, at least a way
of getting back our lives as they had been. I think
I'd learned a thing or two. Surprised myself
to find how much I really cared.

Learned it again that time after the accident.

Even now, and it's six years ago last week,
I shudder to recall that night. I'd had a few drinks, true;
I knew I shouldn't drive. She'd had only the one,
one white. She knew that she'd be driving home.

A rotten night, wind lashing through the trees,
Rain that must have blinded her.
So when she saw
the headlights coming at her,
it's no wonder that she swerved.
I woke up just in time to see us
heading for the tree.

And hear her scream.
'I'm sorry, Francis.'

It still shocks me – that she said sorry.
Whereas if I had had the sense to stop
after one drink, who knows?
If I'd been driving, maybe …
So who's the one who should be feeling sorry?

She didn't wake again.
They had her on the life support for quite some time.
I think I always felt that it was possible
that one day she might still –

I spent those weeks beside her, held her hand,
and talked. Remembered, reminisced,
made wild and hopeful plans I knew
would never happen.

I even prayed. Not sure exactly why,
or whom I was addressing.
Not much anticipation of an answer either,
and of course there wasn't one.
Told her we'd come back here again,
to Oberammergau, the way we'd always said.
A time when we were happy.

But just that still white face, no flicker even.
Brain dead, they said.

They waited many weeks. They watched me there,
day in, day out. A curious time, oddly happy even,
a time of such togetherness as we had never known.
I thought one day how she'd have liked the fact
that I was there at last as she had always wanted.
An irony of life.
Or death.

At last they made it clear.
The pointlessness of waiting.
The decision that was mine.
They all said their goodbyes.
Few tears by now.
The girls had cried them out, and
Richard's he had kept for private times.

And then we were alone, as I had wanted.
A simple matter, so it seems, to end a life.

I wanted just one miracle, one moment at the end,
when possibly her eyes might flicker,
she might see me there,
and know that at the end I had been there with her.
For that I prayed.

I kept my eyes on hers, waiting for that instant
when all machines would stop,
the final beat of heart be registered.
Waiting, as I'd asked, alone.

But then I knew the door behind me opened.
I turned, an instant only, to see
who had intruded, a nurse who shook her head
apologetically, retreated.
I turned back. Too late.
The end had come, and it was over.
I had, as always, not been there.

So much to be forgiven. This promise is, at least,
one I can keep. There's nothing that I hope for,
nothing I'm expecting,
but I have come, as we had planned.

No matter if this time there's someone else
who'll sit beside me at the play.
A very different type.

Her expectations will not be the same as Pam's.
And I won't face the careful plans of friends
and their manipulations, so well meant.

We both have learned our limitations
over years, and can foresee a future
in a comfortable union. No demands.

Meanwhile our superficial conversation rattles on.
I'm sorry if you wonder why I would avoid
your question, and prefer to keep
our talk about wine markets, and their seasons.

Life is full of times and seasons, a lesson
that I learned too late.
I wish that I had earlier understood
the changing world around us.
That time moves on,
and will not wait our pleasure.

Caroline

I'm talking to them, Rob, as you suggested.
But it's not easy going.
I'd swear the man I spent
the last part of the evening with was sure
that I was coming on to him.
Not my type at all. We both know,
you must know, my darling,
exactly what type I come on to . . .

I'd wanted to make this an email to remind you
how much we can mean to each other.
But I won't. Maybe tomorrow.
Tonight I'm going to my solitary bed,
and missing you.

In any case, there was a nightmare scream
that came from next-door's room. I wondered
if I should go to knock, see if she's alright.
She seems a very private non-forthcoming woman,
headmistress, I think, of some big college.
Someone said the friend whom she was
travelling with had died quite recently.
Strange that she's still here with us,
but then you never know what people do.
I never know what I would do
without you in my life.

Good night, my darling love.

ELINOR: THE PRIORESS'S TALE

Ther was also a Nonne, a Prioresse ...
... ful plesaunt, and amiable of port.
And peyned hir to countrefete chere
Of court, and been estatlich of manere
And to ben holden digne of reverence.

৩৩

There was also a Nun. A Prioress ...
Pleasant and friendly in all her ways, and straining
To counterfeit a courtly kind of grace.
A stately bearing fitting to her place,
And to seem dignified in all her dealings.

Shut out the impact of the dream!
Did I cry out aloud? But even if I did
who would there be to hear?

This building's old; the rooms are large;
the walls are solid. It's not a gimcrack
extravaganza of a modern architect,
complete with polished surfaces,
designer details, discreet touches
of sophisticated elegance. If I can
focus on the building, concentrate
on just how much this nineteenth century
solidity, assertiveness, is mirror
of its age, perhaps it might be possible
to once again obliterate her face.

Did I cry out? I know I reached across
the huge expanse of bed, mocked by
the emptiness of snowy linen –
a testament to German *Hausfrau*'s arts –

thinking still to feel her body there,
soft and warm and pliable, so familiar
to my seeking arms. But no one there.

Looming walls of stone, each side,
they tower above me. I see, I feel
my small self dwarfed. I hurry fearful
down the narrow road they border.
It's night. On either side they menace.

So what if anyone had heard? Just one more
foolish woman having nightmares …

Whose job to check on me? Perhaps
another role for tour guides? 'If any in your
group shows signs of night disturbance,
be prepared to offer reassurance.'
A cautious knock and query at the door,
especially with females of a certain age,
inclined to night hysteria, you know.

A woman of a certain age? I've seen them
so described in tabloids and in magazines
that specialise in tales of sex, sensation,
violence, melodrama. 'A certain age?'
What age protects one from the feelings
that lie behind that word? I wish I knew.

It would be good to have a certainty
that there would come a time I too
might be so safely past emotions that can
bring such danger with them. A woman
of my age may not have reached that stage.

For risk avoidance has become so much
my way of life – hard to contemplate
a mode of operating that's without the need

to keep a watchful eye, make choices
that reduce the dangers of a backlash that could
spell the end of such a promising career.

Choices – what is life without such choices?
The moment that she came to me and said
that willingly she'd sacrifice it all –
husband, money, social status, reputation,
everything – to be with me. That for her,
greatest happiness lay in my arms …
if I would make a similar choice …

Put it away! That memory is still too raw.
I cannot face it now.

Looming walls of stone, each side,
they tower above me. I see, I feel
my small self dwarfed. I hurry fearful
down the narrow road they border.
It's night. On either side they menace.

Think back instead to better times.
To all the years together.
Vagrant fleeting scraps, suited to a night
of fits and starts of dreams and nightmares.
Like many others now that she has gone.

Tonight so fresh, so real. Tonight in Munich
where we should have been together,
the first night of a time she'd coveted,
a tour she'd wanted many years. 'We'll start – '
said with such a would-be blasé air
that made me, irritated, turn away,
' – just like the medieval pilgrims did, and
travel several days, to Oberammergau.'

For all pretences of sophistication,
a child's excitement shone through in her eyes.

I tried, I'll swear I tried, to enter willingly
her world of faith – religiosity, I'd call it –
but always with a half-raised brow
and careful monitoring of contempt.

'We start with a first day in München.'
Enough to make me grit my teeth,
that phony German accent, vain attempt
to sound a linguist, from one whose
Anglo tongue impeded any sounds
of authenticity, no matter how she tried.

'Don't do it!' I'd said once, in early years.
'You sound so fake.' The welling tears
and trembling lips that struggled hard
to laugh away my words taught me
a lesson that I tried hard to remember.

'You know so much,' that tremulous voice,
'I only want to keep up with you, and not seem
uneducated in your company.' Oh Kitty,
what is education when it's weighed
against the love you gave so generously?
I am as trapped in nightmares day as night.

Looming walls of stone, each side,
they tower above me. I see, I feel
my small self dwarfed. I hurry fearful
down the narrow road they border.
It's night. On either side they menace.

Her nickname. How it lasted through the years.
They called her that at school, I can remember.
Some years behind me, as she was, but still
I can recall the child whom even teachers
knew as Kitty, never Catherine. It seemed to fit
the cute and cuddly little girl she was.

A curious child, with penchants
for the older girls, who made a pet of her.
Within the closed world of a boarding school,
one needed smaller creatures
to love and cosset. She was ours.
But always, tacitly acknowledged,
I was the one her heart belonged to.
And her claws. For kitten-like, she'd scratch
when her beloved seemed attacked.

Remember now her tears, so freely falling,
when, school days over,
without grief I departed, left her, free.

She wrote and telephoned,
and begged to meet, continue friendship.
Quite undaunted by my silence,
she persisted, while I, bemused by all the glamour
of new life in a heady world of lectures,
seminars, debates, of minds that met –
and bodies also – paid no attention
to the voice behind the words I read
and fast discarded.
So finally they stopped.
I heard that she'd left school
and found a job. If anything,
a vague relief. She had been tedious.
Now, in the night,
the memories come crowding.

She'd married well, I realised, when next we met.
A school reunion, I recall.
I felt her eyes on me,
from where she sat, petite, serene,
and garbed, I recognised, in clothes
that I had seen in small boutiques
where price tags seemed inverse

to sizes of establishment,
and only mirrored reputation.

No longer such a kitten – now a well-fed cat,
sleek and cared for, I could see.
'Who's that?' I asked the woman next to me,
old and trusted friend of former years,
a lover briefly, mutual affection still.
She peered, short-sightedly.

'Oh, Kitty. You remember?
She had a crush on you at school.'

I looked again. 'Done pretty well, I'd say,
and come up in the world.'

Always a mine of gossip,
my former love now gave a pithy overview
of Kitty's life and marriage.
Property developer, her man,
and big-time too. Kitty often in the social pages.

'Not that you ever read them,' she observed,
affectionately. 'You wouldn't know.'
I smiled. We were old friends.
Then Kitty came towards us.

A new start to my life.
So casual, the way it all began.

Kitty's voice, the same voice I remembered,
a little tentative. 'I've always hoped we'd meet again.
You had such influence on me. Way back, I mean.'

I smiled. 'You look as if your life has turned out well.'

'And yours. I watched how your career developed.
You must have been the youngest woman ever
to get the job as principal of Morningside.'

Her tone was almost reverential.
Of course it's true. I was the youngest.
I was flattered that she knew.
Not too surprising, looking back.
Newspapers and the women's magazines
had made a story of it.
The council was delighted. 'All good PR,'
A solemn portly chairman told me.
'Go for it, my dear girl. The more publicity
we get, the better. Great for our image.
You're young, progressive,
graduate of Oxbridge, and good to look at too.'
Nothing like the gallantry of aging council chairs.

I thought again how wise I'd been
to keep my private life apart.
Doubtful I'd have had even an interview
if they had known just how
my cautious life was organised.
In truth, most often kept repressed.
No sense in taking risks that could be
easily avoided. But I confess,
it pleased me Kitty knew of my success.

Success comes at a price, and I'd earned mine.
Those years of work, the dedicated hours of study,
determined sacrifice of pleasures that in time
have brought me to this point are not begrudged
because they gave me what I wanted.

Life's only sacrifices really are the ones
that don't reward with their aimed-for objective,
a point too often overlooked.
My persona, then, the public face
so carefully constructed,
could not be called a sacrifice of self,
because it gave me the respect I craved.

One does not get a five year contract,
that safeguard for employing bodies,
renewed each time it's due,
reliably foreseen, unless one is delivering
what has been expected.
And what the indicators?
Clients satisfied: a parent body that sings praises
in the public world; a student population
that brings home the bacon – crude but true –
with academic honours and a record of successes
that wins community respect. Respect –
the way my girls feel about me.

I've tried to analyse it through the years, just
what it is they feel. Part admiration, that I know.
They check my clothes, my shoes, my hair –
they rate my level daily, with approval.
But with a healthy fear of what has been
my cultivated skill in scathing words.

It's little wonder that the parents say,
with scarcely veiled ambivalence,
Miss Kirby really knows just how
to manage teenage girls. They little realise
how fully I can understand girls' other lives.

The language that they use among themselves,
the drink, the drugs, the active sexuality
that makes their real world different from
the cautious picture they present an adult viewer.

I comprehend, far better than they'll ever know,
complicit private lives. For that is mine also.
I stand before them in assemblies, knowing
what they see, with half-reluctant admiration.
A woman poised, successful, elegant, sufficient
to herself. They speculate, I'm sure, in idle moments,

just where my satisfactions lie, but there are men,
the friends of many years, who can provide
protective colouration when it's needed.

How Kitty hated that. How sometimes
with a conscious cruelty I'd comment lightly
on pleasures of a night she had not shared.

'Why not?' I'd needle casually. 'After all,
you have your Leonard. Why not admit
that I too can have others in my life?'
But even as I did, I knew the truth of it,
the quick flick of the whip to bring about
the quiver of her lip,
assurances that he meant less to her than me,
assurances I knew were true, however slight
their value to me. Why then persist?

I've asked myself this question often; still
no answer comes. Not in these nights.

Looming walls of stone, each side,
they tower above me. I see, I feel
my small self dwarfed. I hurry fearful
down the narrow road they border.
It's night. On either side they menace.

All very well to salve my conscience
with the thought that I did not begin it.
I chose to let it happen.

Those early days of tentative beginnings
could quite easily have been avoided.
First coffees, then the casual dinners –
I knew, although she may have been less sure,
exactly where this friendship led.

She had a curious innocence, unlikely
as it seemed, and when I queried idly how
her husband felt about the time she spent with me,
her tone was unconcerned.
'Oh, Leonard's gone so much.
His work takes him away. I'm sure
that there are other women in his life.'

'It doesn't bother you?' I was nonplussed,
but Kitty's face was open.

'Our life in bed has always been a non-event,
I've felt. I guess it's put him off.'

In some ways guileless as a child, in others
so experienced. The first nights that we spent –
the weekend interstate to see an exhibition,
the wandering through the gallery careful
not to touch, but each of us aware of what
the night would bring …
the naked hunger of her lips, her seeking body,
while mine already leapt in unanticipated wish
to meet her needs …
I had not known that I could love like that.

In midnight hours I can recall too vividly
those early years, the passion of our meetings,
the careful assignations and the desperation
of the times apart.

Shared secret lives, but always cool facades
of casual friendship in social gatherings.
Yet eyes, that met across a room,
and lingered just a shade too long,
in mutual awareness of the time to come,
when we would once more

fold ourselves into each other's arms
and lie, our bodies twined, in pleasures shared.

At times, I tried to stand aside,
to see, to analyse, just wherein lay this feeling.
Was it the satisfaction
of shared delights in bed,
or just the thrill of feeling
so adored, so loved, so wanted?

I knew her as a shallow silly creature,
her world so limited, her sphere
of fashion shows and restaurants,
of money-raising charities – the substitute
for children that she could not bear –
her simple child-like faith
that roused my irritation –
all these I knew,
and yet in spite of all my mind deplored,
yet still my body flew to hers,
still I would feel the deep protective tenderness
that welled in spite of all.
And how she loved me! Just for that all else
could be forgotten. In darkest nights this haunts me.

Looming walls of stone, each side,
they tower above me. I see, I feel
my small self dwarfed. I hurry fearful
down the narrow road they border.
It's night. On either side they menace.

When did it end? When did I first become
aware that all those qualities
that once delighted me
now irked and irritated,
for fondness had become a tolerance
that had to be maintained?

I struggle now to find the moment that marked
   separation.
It eludes me. Subtly it began.
The sense of boredom in our time together,
the increase in annoyance I battled to conceal.
The frequency with which I started
to find reasons not to be available …

Not hard to find.
The pressures of my daily life were mounting
as the years went by. The school itself
a greater burden as it grew –
they say, and rightly, there's nothing that succeeds
quite like success. I proved it true.
Enrolments grew; complexities they generated
made many days exhausting.

Easy to plead obligations that Kitty too could
   understand –
or made pretences of.
Crises abounding. Lean years when governments
cut grants to private schools. Campaigns for raising
   funds
for those facilities that kept us so attractive to the
   parents
whom we courted. The damping of potential scandals
like cyber-bullying – we found it rampant in our juniors,
those well-bred students we admitted to our halls
from upper-classes, our elite, our clientele.

'Ice Lady' … my persona stood me in good stead.
(Oh yes, I'd always known my nickname with the girls.)

In early years it bothered me. I understood
that they had seen the contrast with my predecessor,
the type of warm and caring figure
they'd learned to love as leader of their school.

Her presence round the campus legendary.
A smile for every girl – their names all known.
Her Sunday entertainments for the seniors …
Her reputation as a woman who was loved by all.
Her style of leadership
a very different one from mine.

But then, her school a small and intimate affair.
Mine four times larger,
and in the forefront of initiatives, success.
I saw my role as public face, administrator,
a CEO. No more those days of principals
as caring mother figures. They're gone.

There was one time, I think, just one,
I found myself considering
'What would she have done?'

I thought of it once more tonight,
when yet again those old familiar dream walls
loomed, and when I found myself as always,
trapped.

It's strange, the years have gone,
but still I see that woman's face
the day I told her she would have to go.
A timid, mouse-like woman,
Heather Smith, I sometimes wondered how
she could be so successful in the classroom,
especially teaching maths, but there it was.
Results were excellent; that's all that matters.

The girls, I think, found her somewhat amusing,
saw her as dog-eyed, tremulous, pathetic,
but knew she was devoted to their learning,
and to them. Especially to the ones like her,
the shy, uncertain ones who needed her support.

I found impressive her sheer dedication,
but felt uneasy at those extra hours,
tutoring with patience girls who needed help.
In lunch breaks, after school,
she made time for them. Always a ready ear,
available to those who found
they could confide their problems to her.

I knew that there were rumours
of her closeness with some senior girls,
but chose to close my ears.
Good maths teachers are hard to find, these days.

But no school can afford a scandal,
and after the first parent came, complaining,
I was forced to act.

She did not try to tell me it was lies.
At least it was all managed without the need
to bring in witnesses, authorities.

'Heather,' I said, 'I must find out the truth.
You understand?'

'I did,' she said, looking side to side,
more like a frightened rabbit than I'd ever seen,
'put my arm round the girl.
She was in tears, a private problem.'

'And that was all? They say she was a favourite
of yours – someone you singled out for favours,
for special private tutoring quite often?'

'She needed help. Her maths was weak.
Her home life also wretched.
A most unhappy girl. I tried to help.'

'She told her parents that you kissed her.
Is that true?'

The woman's face went scarlet, and her hands,
always a giveaway, scrabbled at her skirt.
'She needed to feel someone ... cared for her.'

The woman who replaced her was brisk and jolly,
but no more private tutoring. Heather I saw
only once more, when she came for a reference.

Of course I did not give it, though she wept,
told me teaching was her life.

I kept myself detached and calm.
'Perhaps you need to find another field ;
a girls' school may not be the place
that's best for you.' The irony was lost on her.

Too dangerous to let emotion rule you –
Heather showed me that.
Was this why times with Kitty were less satisfactory?
Yet I was fond of her, and felt
that special tenderness one always has for former loves.
I'll swear she did not guess; her love stayed constant.

Guilty! It made me feel I owed her something.
Something proportionate.
A compensation for my loss of love.

Was this what led me to agree
to such an ill-considered plan,
to use my precious long-anticipated leave
(why do they call it Study Leave?
The sort of euphemism councils so delight in!)
and yield to Kitty's pleas
that we might go away together?

'But Leonard?' I protested weakly.
Swiftly over-ruled.

'He's all in favour,' Kitty's voice was bright,
its firmness out of character.
'He says I need a holiday.
He knows we're friends. Well,'
and again that irritating giggle,
'not exactly how we're friends.'

I winced, but it was true.
While every fibre in me screamed
'Don't do it! No!'
I heard my craven voice say 'Yes,'
and tried to show enthusiasm for the planning.
I think she was convinced.
Her foolish loving face that night is still fixed in my
    mind.

Looming walls of stone, each side,
they tower above me. I see, I feel
my small self dwarfed. I hurry fearful
down the narrow road they border.
It's night. On either side they menace.

I know myself enough to understand just why
tonight the dream has come again.
Wounds re-opened bleed again.
That woman, Irmgard, the tour guide.
Her sympathetic presence and her cautious words.
'We are so sorry that your friend's not here.
If you prefer, we can make changes for you –
You may now like to have a single room. We were,
however, pleased that you decided still to come
and take the tour with us.' I tried to end
the conversation quickly, 'I felt I should,'
and turned away.

But found myself beside another,
a younger woman, some sort of travel writer.
Inquisitive. 'You were to be here with a friend?'

'She couldn't come,' I said dismissively,
and went to bed. I knew that I would dream.

Before I slept, I thought again, 'But why?
Why have I come?' It would have been so easy
to have fled the past, packed up my baggage,
real and otherwise, and made a merciful retreat …
It's not my way. Or is it that I feel I owe her this?
Self-flagellation comes in many forms.

Most often, I can wake myself and thus escape the walls.

But not this time.

Tonight, I stay locked in the dreamscape of my mind,
forced to continue down the path.
But soon the route diverges;
two roads to go, but both hemmed in
on either side.
Pygmy like, I hurry on, more desperate,
lost in Wonderland, knowing
there is somewhere I should be.
Roads open on to roads; huge shadows
from the sentinel cliffs shroud the confusion
of side tracks that offer other routes
to lead me – where? To exit gates?
Or only deeper in this maze
where I am trapped, a dwarfish creature?

Which ones to take? White Rabbit that I am,
I check my watch. I shall be late, I say.
To whom?

I look beside me, and it's Kitty with me,
her eyes reproachful. 'You told me,' she is saying,
'You told me you had checked the route.'

I am defensive. 'So I did. I walked it earlier.
Yesterday I knew. It all looks different now.'

The monstrous walls are menacing, oppressive.

'You should have had this planned.
You never think of me. It's always you.'

I protest fiercely. 'I did. It's just that
everything has changed.'

Where have I heard those words? Where did I speak
    them?

Italy?

The six weeks she had planned,
myself the acquiescent bystander ...
the four weeks that we travelled, both of us
reluctant to admit what every day made clear.
This time disaster for us both.

Each passing day a growing tension,
each night a disappointment.
Lying hostile, separated more by misery than distance.
Unhappiness for her, with my antipathy at most half
    hidden.
For nothing's colder in the grave than a dead love.
This trip the final coup de grâce.

Increasingly her desperate efforts
in day hours once again to find old happiness
we'd known, to wring from me a gesture of affection,

a reminiscence of a better time. The nights …
frustration, desolation, my impatience, guilt.

I should have left. But how to leave her there?
The four day tour to Oberammergau, the culmination
of our time, and still to come? Unthinkable,
though oh so near to irresistible, to leave her there,
to finish this trip on her own.
Another wrong road chosen,
always from the best of motives.
At least, the lesser evil, so I thought.

'I would leave Leo, everything, to be with you.
You know that. Even now.'

We sit in silence on the cliff top for a time,
looking out. Italian coast-line with its sea
of such improbability.
How can there be a blue so deep, so utterly
unfathomable? So beautiful, so dangerous.

'Let's walk,' I say abruptly. 'I can't sit here
and talk about this now.'

But she's insistent, loud, hysterical.
'Yes now! I can't go on like this.
Not after everything we've been.
I've spent my whole life waiting for you.
You have to want to be with me
the way it used to be.
Otherwise there's nothing left.'

I walk ahead, and do not speak.

'I could make things quite difficult for you.'

I wheel around and stare. She's never threatened this.

'A few words here and there. Your life would change.'

We've stopped. A single bird wheels down the cliff face,
dropping to that sea, so deep, impenetrable.

'Would you do that?' I ask her quietly.

She hesitates, then shakes her head
and whispers. 'No. But tell me,
why? What have I done?'

There is no answer I can make.

'It's just – ' there are no words to say –
'that everything … has changed.'
My word is like a knell.
She knows it.
So do I.

And suddenly, impossibly, she's gone.

'But why?' asks Leonard, when he comes to claim her
    body.
'You must know, Elinor. Her emails sounded happy.'

'She slipped,' I tell him evenly. 'She wanted to look over.
There was a bird that flew down to the sea.
She slipped.'

It's fortunate for me that the Italian family further down
the cliff path had seen us standing well apart.
Quite separate.
It saved the possibility of any questions;
they had seen her fall. No culpability on my part,
they were clear.
What irony.

Looming walls of stone, each side,
they tower above me. I see, I feel
my small self dwarfed. I hurry fearful
down the narrow road they border.
It's night. On either side they menace.

Tonight in dreams I wandered through the maze
    of streets,
with Kitty once more at my side.
She asks a question,
quite irrelevant, as hers so often were.
'Did you remember raincoats and umbrellas?'

So typical. I answer,
'It doesn't look like rain.'

At once the heavy spots begin to fall, and we are
climbing upwards in the narrow networked streets.
Till, at the top, we find an opening in the high blank
    walls.
Inside, some steps, and at the top a ledge. We sit,
a little shelter from an overhanging roof, waiting
for the rain to stop.

'You should have thought ahead,'
she says again, 'and brought umbrellas.
You never think of me.'

Huge dream-time clouds,
black and thunderous,
loom close above us.

She leans across, to look below.
'Be careful, Kitty. Could be dangerous.'

She turns to me, and laughs, begins to slip.

I reach for her – but this is where the dream
tonight has ended. So still I do not know.

When I reached out
was it to hold?

Or did I push?

DAY 2

TRAVELLING

Munich –

Oberammergau

Caroline – morning

Morning. A restless night.
I tossed and turned, but not disturbed
by any further cries from other rooms.

Half hoping for a call, a text, an email
in response to mine. But nothing.

Call him? With what excuse?

It's midnight there. He'll be with her.

No quicker way to sever bonds between us.

So. Dress with care. A grey, foreboding day.
No summer weather this. It fits my mood.

To breakfast, then we start our day.
This morning's tour of Munich –
perhaps my chance to talk,
to get to know these people.

STEPHEN: THE SCHOLAR'S TALE

A Clerk ther was of Oxenford also,
That un-to logic hadde longe y-go ...
Of studie took he most cure and most hede.
Noght o word spak he more than was need.

There was an Oxford Cleric too, a student,
Long given to Logic, longer than was prudent ...
His only care was study, and indeed
He never spoke a word more than was need.

I don't know why they drag us on these tours!
A sense of obligation? To make the trip worthwhile?

I look around the others, wondering
whether this is really what they wanted –
a guided tour of Munich.

They all seem acquiescent, even pleased,
to find themselves like cattle,
herded to the bus, then marched
from tourist spot to tourist spot,
in spite of drizzling rain.

I feel the quick sardonic grin
flicker across my face when Irmgard
raises high her green umbrella,
marshals us, her subjects –
victims, should I say? –
to pavements where we stand forlorn
beneath the dripping trees.

'This is,' she tells us, model of Teutonic patience
and precision, holding up that damned umbrella,

'my guide for you. This you must watch
and follow through the streets.
Please not to linger.'

We forbear to comment that to follow
just one green umbrella in the rain
might prove a task beyond our capabilities.
But still, obedient and compliant,
we trudge to see the sights
of this bedraggled rain-swept town.
A bonus tour, they have assured us earnestly,
before our bus sets out for Oberammergau.

I'm not a man for tours.
Nor for these group affairs.

'You really don't like people, do you!'
That had been her accusation – one more
among the many – before she left me ... finally.
There'd been a few departures earlier.
But always in the past she'd found a reason to return.

This time was different, and I knew it.

The things she said were cutting, but quite true.
I'm happier by far when working in my lab.
There people are no complication.
It makes me wonder why I'd married her at all.
Yet early on my work had seemed to interest her;
Perhaps she saw herself the adjunct to a famous man?

For certainly the bright light of those early years,
developments and break-throughs, prestige
of awards they gave me, all created
an allure that must have had appeal. It's hard
to see why else she had pursued me.

'I'd like to interview you for my magazine ...'

That was how it started.
I think her vision of a scientist
was far more glamorous than my reality.
A small and scruffy figure
must have made her wonder,
but then the accolades my work was getting
gave me bonus points, I guess.

I'd never bothered much with women.
For others, girlfriends seemed to come and go.
Too much distraction from their work,
too much time wasted; it should have been
invested in the patient trial and error of experiments
that might or might not lead to further knowledge.

For there ahead it always lay. The moment
that we sought when we might see
the wonder drug, the holy grail.

It was my life. My waking, sleeping, living,
breathing moments all were focused on this goal.
The long night watches in the lab paid off;
painstaking hours alone, well after
fellow-workers had departed for their homes,
their wives, and I was left in peace,
my happiest times.
The glory of those moments when I knew
my instincts right, results that validated what I tried.
Successes came, enough to gain me credit, honour,
prizes and awards, enough to gain me Chloe
with her breathless wide-eyed admiration of my work.

Until she realised that she could not compete,
that even as I lay there in her arms
my heart, attention, brain were elsewhere.
Not surprising she would turn away,
to lie hard-faced towards the wall.

So, freed, I'd slip from the enmeshing sheets,
and quietly return to where I wished to be.

A sense of nothing more, though unacknowledged,
just relief when she admitted finally
it was no use, and left me to my life.

I draw back from these people.

Hard to understand
how I allowed myself to get involved in this.
I'd heard about it, certainly. Who hasn't heard
of Oberammergau? But certainly no interest
in the place. One needs some sort of faith
to come to this event. My only faith is science.
She's a mistress who will tolerate no competition.

So when that woman joined me last night at the bar,
and asked what brought me on this tour,
it would have been embarrassing to tell her
just what a chance event it was.
How my old friend –
one of the few from student days in Düsseldorf –
had pressed his ticket on me, when we met
last week in Stockholm. 'I can no longer go.
You say you have some free days here
before return. So use my ticket.'

Why did I accept?

Even that I'm having trouble comprehending.
A sudden whim?
A scientist does not succumb to sudden whims.
For we are cool and calculating characters,
who weigh decisions,
look carefully at pros and cons,
establish the criteria by which to plan next steps.

But I have seen before how suddenly
the swift leap of intuitive flash can lead one forward.
This journey may be one for me.

One should distrust these flashes. This I've learned
at costs the world does not yet know. And hopefully,
will never know.

I do not seek the peace of the confessional.

There was an irony that only I would comprehend
last night: a man came to me at the Welcome –
'welcome'! They little knew just how unwelcome
such a gathering was to me – then he,
a lean bald-headed man, round and rimless glasses,
came to me where I stood solitary, surveying
drinkers at the bar with cautious cataloguing eye,
identifying types among my fellow travellers.

Brought his glass of wine, a cheap indifferent brand,
and leaned towards me saying that he knew me,
had heard me speak at conferences,
read my papers in the journals.
And how deserved was the award
that I had just received. He was a doctor too,
so he impressed on me, in case I thought
I might be dealing with mere curiosity,
or a celebrity pursuer. Assured me of his interest
in my field. He had had patients
who would profit from my work.

Excuses made, I left the gathering speedily.
Promised myself today to keep away from him.
Tempting, almost, to tell him the truth.

We follow Irmgard and the green umbrella,
as she guides her flock through intermittent showers

down streets that are perhaps less packed
with sight-seers than usual.

Munich.
This place of monks, of wealth through salt,
this city, product of the vision of that Ludwig
who imagined here an 'Athens of the North' –
our heads are stuffed with history
until, like overloaded schoolboys,
we can take no more.

Another irony – our bus now takes us past
the Königsplatz, so based on Greek ideals,
its model the Acropolis, but found itself
the home of Nazi life in Hitler's Germany.

Since the award, I have become
much more aware of ironies in life.

And this the greatest one, that everywhere we go
I find there's plagiarism. They all, we all,
exploit the work of others. Copyists all.

I nod, as Irmgard tells us of the Nymphenburger Palace,
its gardens copy of Versailles, work of imported experts,
of gardeners from that masterpiece of France.
So too its Grand Canal, complete with gondolas,
a Venice brought to southern Germany.

But they at least acknowledged that they copied;
that they borrowed others' work.
Borrowed? Stole?
A grace I did not learn.

So Wilhelm Meister died as he had lived, obscure,
unknown and poor, while I took all the credit
that he should have had.

But now it haunts me.
I am the thief who shrugs his shoulders,
justifies his acts, but can no longer
see his mirrored face without recoil.

She is a jealous mistress, Science;
I learned to give her full respect.
There was no place I felt
at home except in her domain.
A child at home, that Christmas I received
my first experimental set I knew I'd found my love.
Schooldays I remember little of –
except for lunchtimes in the lab,
always the science monitor,
after school unwilling to go home.

Intoxication of the Bunsen burners, pipettes,
microscopes and filter flasks, evaporating dishes,
crucibles and tongs, test tubes and desiccators,
their very names were music to my ears.
I knew my future even then. No clothes
as satisfying as the white lab coat.
No joy as great as the precision
of experiments that gave outcomes
one was seeking.
Was this perhaps where it began?
A love not of enquiry, but obsession with results?

Surely it's results that count.
Incessantly the question beats its tom-tom in my mind.
For if results are not the fundamental issue,
then my own life is empty, hollow,
the mockery I fear.

These Germans understood results.

I look around me, and the question gets its answer
as we travel. The bus that we've been herded on
takes us through streets, past sights
that tell us the same thing.

For even Adolf Schicklgruber got results,
before the madness of his Hitler days took over.
The workers blessed the building projects, autobahns,
that brought them hope in the Depression years,
till megalomania destroyed his mind.

And took this country into madness with him.

We pass the Victory Gate,
then through the arch see the Field Marshall's Hall,
a grim reminder of the way men's dreams
become their downfall.

Mine too? The aims, the goals, so good.
But then, the means?

I look around me in this bus.
I've managed to repel
by force of will so far the company of others.
I have no wish to share the general pairing up of strays
which tours like this engender.

The rain is dampening spirits,
but Irmgard's smile stays fixed.
She knows the duties of a guide.
Her patter is incessant as the rain.
Stories galore, and sights to match.
Each one a message for me.

We pass the sights of Munich, all its glories,
past and present. Three gods are honoured:
sport finds apotheosis in the Stadium,
Olympics feat of steel and plexiglass;

nearby Jevohah's Witnesses find god in Kingdom Hall.
But these rub shoulders with the triumph of our age,
and BMW is home to deities we recognise,
those sleek fast cars.

'A pity,' Irmgard grieves, 'about this rain.'
We cannot see what has been promised.
The building's windows, she informs us,
are sprayed with gold dust to keep out the sun.
A sight to wonder at.
Beat gold with gold, I ponder.
Yet another irony.

The sights roll by; as always it's too much.
Oktoberfest at Teresienplatz? I yawn.
Beer drinking crowds have never had appeal.
More interesting to my mind is Ludwigstrasse,
its sprawling university, the monumental Library,
but I recoil at steady camera snapping of the sights
by avid gaping figures on this bus.

'I've never loved the human race ...' –
a line some poet – Raleigh? – wrote, remembered
from my schooldays, most other things forgotten.
'I've never loved its silly face.' So it continues.

I can relate. How could the feeble antics of these fools
compete with the delights of knowledge? For this
will always take preeminence above inanities,
banalities, the foolish acts of man. And woman!

He never understood that, Wilhelm Meister.

I'd had such hopes of him when first he joined our team.
Young and enthusiastic, dedicated even,
and with that spark, that flash,
which I have seen in just a few
and always yearned for.

Oh, I got results, I know.
I've had the honours and the glory that they bring.
But got them through the sheer painstaking labour
of the hours, the days, the weeks –
even the years.

But he was one of those who saw through fogs
of trivia, minutiae, laborious accumulation
of facts and figures, the painstaking repetition
of experiments and trials that led too often to dead ends.

Then in a moment of sheer inspiration,
his mind would like a conjurer's
make sudden twists, connections,
to take him down new paths I had not seen,
cut through the thickets of the detail
and emerge into a sunny space beyond.

No sunny spaces for us here. The rain still falls,
until we disembark, bedraggled but obedient,
to trail our guide through Munich's sodden streets.

This human flock now gathers and stands docile
clustered round our shepherd, where she raises
one stern directing hand. We gaze with due attention
where she points. A mini-lecture now on Mozart,
and the plaque that tells us of his time in Munich.

'You knew that he was here?'
Irmgard's tone is sharp.
She would have made a schoolmistress, I feel.
Perhaps she has been one, for other people
seem to have had so many lives. It's not my way.
We shake our heads.

'*Idomeneo* had its first performance here in Munich.'

The sheep all look impressed. I'd swear that even if
they might have heard of Mozart, few would know
this was an opera. Mozart.
Another wunderkind, another Wilhelm Meister?
For Willi also had youth on his side,
while I ... my time was passing
and I knew that all these bright young men
would soon outstrip my work.

If he was Mozart, should I see myself
his Salieri? I understand too well the envy
that one feels when, plodding slowly on the track,
one sees the meteoric rise of youth and genius.
For Salieri had served music and his god
as faithfully as I had spent my life
in search of truths that only science offers.
And Salieri knew the bitterness
of finding all he offered spurned, and failing
in comparison with what his rival could produce.

Oh yes, this I could understand. So if he sought
to bring about the downfall of the other,
with that too I can empathise.
Or more than empathise.

An odd word, that. Not one I often use.
Few people anywhere whose feelings
I would wish to share.

Another thing I could not understand
in Willi. At times I'd find him watching me,
a look I failed to read. Exasperated,
once I asked what he was staring at.

He reddened – almost like a girl, his blushes –
and apologised. Told me how much he'd learned
from working with me,
but wondered why I never talked of outcomes.

Never seemed to want to know
how what we did would make a difference
to those who waited desperately
for what we might achieve.

'I can't afford,' I told him crisply, 'to let myself
be side-tracked by these things.'

He looked surprised, but then he always was
a bleeding heart. Weekends he was a volunteer,
I'd heard, who worked with crippled children.
That time, I felt, would have been spent
more profitably in the lab.
For Willi Meister had potential,
though I writhe to say it, to be great.

I felt no envy for his youth, his looks, his charm,
for he had all of these, it's true.
But he had more.

They talk of genius in speaking of musicians,
artists, writers, poets – there is another genius
which lives in those whose minds, precise and subtle,
probe, analyse, dissect the world I know.

Our tools are not ephemera of words and notes;
our palettes are not paints;
the metals that we deal with are not fashioned
as objects for adornment or the eye's delight.
For us the intricacies lie within
the possibilities of teasing out their mysteries
of combination, the secrets that they hold,
the truths they may reveal.

Old adages still have their point:
if genius is largely perspiration,
and inspiration only a small strand,
my excellence is based on years

of slow painstaking work.
But Willi's?

No, he had that spark of genius,
that sudden flash of insight that would take him
into fields that we, the drones,
had never contemplated.

He'd worked on something, quietly, alone.
'Not yet,' his answer when I asked.
'I'll tell you when I'm sure.' He saw my doubts.
'But if I'm right, this will be big. It just might be
what we have waited for. So many people out there
who await this too. But first I must be sure …'

I plodded on in growing desperation.
Failure built on failure. Each one
eliminating possibilities.
The way, I told myself, that all good research goes.
But always with unease, that grew as time went by.

One day he came to me, and with shy pride,
showed me what he was doing.
'I think,' his voice was tentative,
'I really think I might be on to something.'

When I recall that moment, the same red mist
swamps everything. All my efforts, all these years,
and here this boy, this child, this stripling
sees a way to go that has eluded me so long.
He laid the data down before me,
an offering, and waited for my words.

'I'll need some time,' I said,
my smile more grimace than approval.
'It's complicated stuff.
Leave it with me.'

He looked crestfallen. 'But can't you see – ?'

I didn't let him finish. 'Tomorrow we can talk it through.'

Tomorrow never came for Willi Meister.
A wet night, and hill roads, a way he had
of roaring round the bends.
Road King, he said his Harley was,
and that's the way he always said he felt.
Unlikely choice, his bike – but then
I never really understood him.
One bend the Road King didn't quite control.

Next morning there was quiet in the lab,
and people spoke in hushed tones of the way
he always had a cheerful smile, a friendly word.
They talked about that more than what I felt important.
The promise that he'd had. But then,
perhaps they didn't know as much about that as I did.

We reach the Marienplatz, and steady rain is falling.
Not deterred, our warden finds us what she terms
a 'pick position.' We wait the magic moment
when the famous clock will strike. Around us
crowds are gathering, regardless of the weather.

The clock hand slowly moves, and there we are.
Eleven. Cameras poised, they wait, umbrellas tilted.
I move a little to avoid the rivulets
that stream from the stout lady next to me.
'*Entschuldigen*,' she beams at me,
teutonic and apologetic.
I try a half smile and avoid her eyes
lest conversation starts.

A ripple stirs expectant crowds as with the striking
of the hour the famous marionettes appear.

To *oohs* and *aahs* we watch the royal group of figures
whose wedding rites are celebrated in this scene.
The jousting knights below fight on,
to music of the glockenspiel, until one falls –
beside me my companion sighs in satisfaction.
The victor is Bavarian. She's happy.
Further down more men rotate ;
Irmgard has told us it's the Coopers' Dance.
Another celebration of the ending of the plague.

That plague had reached a natural end;
no need of men like me – or Willi –
to develop antibodies, vaccines, cures.
They had their leeches, cupping, and their prayers.

And Oberammergau remains. Their ten year tribute
to the god that they believed had showed them mercy.
I've never wondered who might give us thanks
for what we have achieved. The finding out is all
that matters to me. What happens after that may be
concern for others, not for me. But here
the coopers prance around in gratitude and joy.

And then it's over. But the crowd waits on.
There's still one last act that we wait for,
knowing it will signify the end of this performance.
The marionettes retreat, doors close,
then at the top the small gold bird appears
and chirps three times. For just a moment
I had thought the bird a cockerel.
Uncomfortably reminiscent, that.
A cock that crows three times?

Yes, betrayal comes to mind.
Betrayal lives too close to surface in my mind.

For Willi had been right; he'd seen,
just as he thought, the way ahead.
And no one knew what he had done but me.

So no one ever knew. The moment last week
when I stepped towards the stage
in Stockholm's Concert Hall
to listen to citations for advances I had made
was gall and wormwood to me.
For where was Willi's name in all of this?
Buried in obscurity
as was the body that his mind inhabited.

Why should I be concerned? It matters little
whose the name on the award; what counts is what
we know now. Yet Willi would have thought more
of the use that would be made of this, one further step
to halt the march of cancer through our times.

Not my concern. I took his work;
he's dead and gone.

My years of effort should have counted.
This was what I deserved
for midnight hours of dedication.
It's only moments when like this –
a bird that sounds three times –
I think again what I have done.

The crowd begins to move. My group disperses
into coffee shops. 'We must meet here,'
our guardian says, 'at one o'clock exactly.
Those who wish may follow me into the church;
It is the Frauenkirche, beautiful.'

The others form themselves into small clusters.
Some look enquiringly at me.

I shake my head, go off alone. The poet's words
return, but this time I remember more exactly
what they were. A scientist should be exact!

'I wish I loved the human race.
I wish I loved its silly face.'

Caroline

An opportunity too good to miss.
They're moving off towards the Frauenkirche,
with Irmgard shepherding decisively.
John looks at me, a wink, a gesture.
Invitation? I shake my head.
My job is here,
to get to know these people.
Despite determined efforts, some of her flock
bypass the church doors, slip discreetly
out of sight across the platz, and make
towards inviting warmth and lights
of little coffee lounges.

I follow, noting the chic belted coat, the heels,
absurd for touring, of the woman
who now turns, and looks invitingly at me.

Inside, reflected in the gleaming glass of mirrors
I study the display in windowed cabinets:
strudels, kuchen, tortes, row on row
of tempting German fare.

We lean back from the table, stirring idly
at our coffees, listening to the clatter
of the crowd around us. She smiles,
and as we chat I find myself absorbed.

ALICIA:
THE WIFE OF BATH'S TALE

A good Wyf was ther of bisyde Bathe ...
She was a worthy woman al hir lyve;
Housbondes at chirche-dore she hadde five,
Withouten other companye in youthe.

୬୨

A worthy woman from beside Bath city ...
A worthy woman all her life, what's more
She'd had five husbands, all at the church door,
Apart from other company in youth.

The biggest leap, I think, my dear,
was number one to number two,
for after that a matrimonial bed
became habitual – and I have always been,
so much, when you come down to it,
a creature ruled by habit.

I see the glint that sparks your eye;
a faint curve of amusement curls your lip
for all your efforts to conceal it.
'A marrying habit?' Words are
clearly hovering in your mouth,
but with a truly laudable control
you are preventing them from being spoken.

Yes, marriage can become a habit,
just like any other. And, after all,
if anyone should know this,
surely I'm the one. Four husbands down the track –
another poised there on the starting blocks –
you must agree that I am qualified

to talk about the state of wedded bliss.
There's nothing like a varied sample
to build up expertise. Oh well, if not quite that,
experience at least.

The gossip columnists have found me
fascinating. As you, I'm sure, well know.
I must admit I recognised your name. In fact
I think that some time in the past
you've interviewed me for a piece
that you were writing for a magazine –
Sydney patrons of the arts, or something
of that sort. So this is not the first time
that our paths have crossed. However,
I suspect you may not want it broadly known
that you are here professionally?

You're not concerned? You're gathering
some background for a book? That's fine!
I've never been a private person, so this
is scarcely a concern to me. Though you
may not find others so accommodating.

Accommodating … Always my strong suit.
One needs to know one's talents – that is mine!
Capacity to recognise the needs of any situation,
as well as those of people in it.
And then a willingness,
almost predisposition,
to satisfy those needs.

It's really no surprise that many men have found
the door to matrimony easy to fling open,
and welcome me inside.
There's no excuse for any woman
wishing to assume the married state
to find herself alone. For after decades

of flirtation with the world of single bliss
most women of intelligence have come to realise
that marriage offers greatest opportunities
for freedom.
By and large, men seek the governing hand:
the woman who is able to disguise the iron fist
and sheath it in a velvet glove will meet their needs.

You raise an eyebrow?
Not so certain of this truth?
But then you've been conditioned by upbringing.

Education, all the messages of media
try to paint a picture of the joys of liberation,
ignoring fundamental truths.
For woman, as for man, the battle of the sexes
is the core of life.

For us, the maintenance of mastery is central.
The happiest of men are those who dimly sense
that deep below the superficial gloss of their machismo
lies yearning to be ruled.
For then they too are free.
They can relinquish all prescriptions
that the world of gender expectations
places on them, and return
to simple pleasures of their childhood days,
laying aside the pressures of responsibility.

You're young. You'll learn the truth of what I say.

You ask me for my evidence?

Consider then my life.
It's evidence enough.
Habituation to the marriage bed
has brought some lessons as the decades passed,
and darling, one day you will see their value.

Like you, I once was trusting, quite deluded.
Believed the promises men made,
and thought the world well lost for love.
I see, your face betrays you.
You haven't passed this stage,
although I must confess surprise.
I would have thought by now
such naïve adolescent innocence destroyed
by the experience your way of life has given.

Strange, looking back.
You're in your twenties, I suspect –
no? Older? You're wearing well, my dear.
At your age I was trusting, too.
Locked into an affair that had not taught me yet
the fundamental truth –
a woman is a fool if she becomes dependent on a man.

Incredible, the cliché that it was.
You must yourself have seen it many times.
Sleeping with the boss!
I look back at the girl I was, a silly child,
so unaware, who thought herself sophisticated,
adult, so mature, who sat at night with candles lit,
and opened wine, and waited for the man
who found himself committed,
not able to leave wife and guests to be with her.

Now, looking back, I find myself amazed
to see the sheer simplicity of mind
that locked me firmly for so many years
into a situation that was so …
conventional? Predictable?
My sisters, all my friends, had lectured me,
and pointed out my folly. But no!
I was so sure that this was right,
that he, so smooth, sophisticated,

one day would leave his wife …
and come to me.

I like to think it was a rare mistake
(a fault of youth) to yield the power to someone else
in a relationship. And only one more time
that I would so misjudge what I should do.
Yet, truth to tell, I'm oddly grateful to him.
Through years with Guy I grew
from simple girlhood and learned lessons
that have stood me in good stead.

Through it all, a common enough tale of woe –
the heart-break of his leaving – came resolution;
I'd set my life course on a different path,
and learn how women should relate to men.

Appearances of compromise, accommodation,
pliancy, but don't engage the heart.
Always maintain a steely independence.
Instinct led me down a track
that has proved advantageous. Like horses,
men to feel the flick of reins, albeit hidden,
and sense that somewhere there's a rider in control.

I'd learned my lesson well. When Solly Mannheim
found himself entranced by what I offered –
youth, firmness of the flesh that must have contrasted
quite poignantly with sagging skin and wrinkles
in the matrimonial bed, indifference of habit
and a body worn by child-bearing and broken nights …
it was not hard to show a breathless interest in his words.

Though paunchy, balding, small, the man was knowing,
so it was easy to become absorbed within his world.
Again I learned – and, like his pearls, accreted knowledge.

For Guy had taught me arts of love, an expert he,
in pleasures of the flesh, a skill acquired that proved
so valuable in years to come, and made it possible
to earn my way from bed to bed.

Another lives also inside my skin –
the girl I stood beside one night
in some hotel, its marbled mirrored ladies' room
capturing reflections of our faces as we chatted,
lipstick in hand, the way we women do. I asked,
as one does at such moments, what she did.

The answer casual, as the question was: a call girl.

'Must be interesting,' my comment,
covering confusion of the moment.

'It is; I simply do for money what many do for free.'

Words that have echoed in my mind
down through the years.
Well, darling, I related to her easily,
for I now do for money – and position –
what many do with much less recompense.
One's talents should be cultivated, honed, then used.

Sol was appreciative, and eager to take full advantage
of what he sensed I might provide.
A few foretastes, a limited offering,
enough to whet an appetite for more.
His aging wife discarded, he was mine.
And, fairly, I was his. A bargain is a bargain.

He got what he had purchased. I too.
I had his name, his money, and his business acumen.
I learned from his experience,
and thus acquired my own.
He said I had an eye for pearls,

a talent for design, and soon he valued this
as much as other skills he still enjoyed.
He taught me well, made me his partner.
I learned to bargain with him
in back alleys in the East, to scrutinise for lustre,
shape, evaluate the weight without recourse to scales.

You didn't know about my business interests?
This does not surprise me, though I thought
in your field some research might well
have told you of my opening nights
for new collections. But then, it's not your area
of interest, I suspect, although the double strand
of baroques in your bracelet must have cost some lover
a fair sum. My dear, you must learn not to blush ...
a girlish habit that charms only in the very young.

All life is learning, and with Sol I learned
accommodations of a different sort.
He found in me a willing partner
who'd satisfy the urges past years taught him
made resort to those with special skills
a need – and payment.

I made discoveries of a different kind.
That sometimes those who seem most dominant
in public life are driven most by private
and opposing needs – I scarcely have to tell you more.

We are both women of the world, I'm sure,
and understand the possibilities of men.
There were returns; within two years
he had established for me several small boutiques.
The years have seen these grow into a healthy chain.
Whatever I gave Sol he has repaid.

I grieved his death, a heart attack ill-timed –
a moment he would not have chosen –
then locked away, with some relief,
the trappings of his pleasures.

But domination comes in different forms;
a subtler kind gives subtler pleasure.
I had not thought to marry yet again,
but there's a calm tranquillity I seek
that's only found within conventions of our social world.
A brief respite of solitude and single bliss sufficed.

But look – this respite too is over. The group returns;
soon we'll be herded yet again onto the bus.
I might have gone with them, although another tour,
in spite of all the Frauenkirche's charms,
has lost appeal. I've seen too many grand cathedrals
in my day. I would have gone compliantly
with Francis, as at first he wanted,
but was spared – his business interests intervened.
A meeting with a wine-maker.

Francis? We plan to marry on return back home.
We're talking pros and cons of matrimony.
It would be my fifth time. But then perhaps,
some habits should be broken?

But that's another story – if you want it,
join me later for a coffee. We'll talk more.

I should have known, foreseen, that talking to you earlier
would so revive the past for me, stir up so many memories,
I'd almost hoped you would not seek me out again,
in spite of what I said.

There's always danger lurking in too much introspection.
Yet strangely fascinating to review one's life,
and see just how the patterns fall.

Of course, the lure of a good listener helps –
and darling, you have clearly worked at being that.
The right degree of rapt attention,
the gently nudging question when the well dries up.
You're good, I'll tell you that.
but I am still uncertain what you want from me.
I somehow doubt it's just the interest of my story.
A model for your future life, or do you think that you
can learn from my mistakes?

All very well to sit and, smiling, shake your head.
I wonder what is going on inside it –
but that is scarcely my concern.
For me you're just convenient,
a sounding board, a chance to ponder on my life,
and try to see which road I follow next.

If there is anyone I miss, it's Number 2 along the nuptial
    track,
for Alex was of all the easiest to talk to. That fits,
of course, for what do lawyers do but sit
and listen to their clients' woes, and try
to sift the grain from chaff?

Accretion yet again – small wonder that I married him.
I had the money, and experience – of many types –
but lacked the things that he could give me:
security and status in the social world.
For this was his milieu,
the world of art and music, galleries and openings,
first nights and festivals, book launches and exotica,
the newest restaurants before discovery by the hoi polloi,

the world of foreign films, some strange, incomprehensible,
but his indulgence was to tutor me to fit within this world.

For all his prowess in the office,
his sharp wits and insights,
his knowledge of the law,
there was a quality
it took me time to recognise.
I'd speculated,
certainly, about his caution,
arm around my shoulders,
friendly kiss upon the cheek,
warmth without passion –
a strange response to one
who always has communicated
her availability.

The night he talked of marriage it was clear
it was a business proposition that he broached.
An invitation that would give me privilege and status,
freedom to live my life exactly as I chose, but
   circumspectly.
He offered me his friendship, his companionship,
no more.

'Are you …?' I hesitated, not sure
whether this was open for discussion.

He answered crisply: 'No, not men.
I simply have no need,
no wish for sex. I'm not alone.
It's a condition more common than you'd think.
But one that I prefer to keep unknown,
and not a matter for my public image.
It's only that I trust you,
and cannot offer marriage under false pretences,
that I tell you now.'

'But you've been married? What of that?'

I knew that he he'd been widowed for at least two years.

'It was the same with her.
A good contented life together;
some pleasures she took elsewhere.'

'Why marry then?'

'I need a hostess, a woman to adorn my table, and my life.
You do this well – already there is friendship, liking –
am I misled?'

I shook my head. 'I need a little time.
This is a strange idea, but certainly it has appeal.'

'I should in fairness add another thing.
It will not be a long arrangement.
My cancer has returned;
this time I can't expect remission.
But don't let this become a factor.
I'm asking for a wife, not nurse.
There'll be professionals,
when that time comes.'

It was a strangely happy marriage;
perhaps the secret is to marry as a friend.
I came to love the life he gave me;
in most things he deferred to me.

Increasingly I came to govern his affairs,
domestic and professional; our lives were rich and full
and with his guidance I now entered worlds
I had not known.
For Alex was Pygmalion, and I his Galatea –
it was his joke, his hobby.
I came to understand it and enjoy the role.

And soon his Galatea had no need of guidance.
Once more I had become free, and so took control.
My other needs I met discreetly.
It isn't hard, if one has money and can be a patron,
to find young men who welcome ...
patronage ...

He died as he had lived, with uncomplaining courtesy,
and thanking me for all that I had done.
A bargain kept on both sides;
we parted with regret.

I think it was at this time that you met me,
an article you'd planned about the role of artists
and their patrons. I rather doubt
the version that I gave you was complete.
You were so very young,
and with a curious innocence I still recall.

So he was Number 2? You're right;
we still have 3 and 4,
and time is running out.
In fact in many ways that's true.

For if one has a general penchant for the older man –
for marriage anyway – one reaches far too fast a stage
when there are not so many hanging ripe for plucking.

I moved quite rapidly from Alex' death to Simon.
His lawyer. It was fitting; we'd come together
in those last months that Alex had.
A comfort to have had an expert in the field,
and someone old, mature.
No brash young Turk with way to make,
a smooth and talented professional,
but this man also seeing ends ahead,
and closing of the doors.

A dedicated man, of human sympathy,
with great capacity for bringing comfort
to the grieving partners cancer sprinkled in his path.

'You could do worse,' said Alex wryly,
when he observed how Simon looked at me.
'It's time you had a life again.'

'Oncology's a grim reminder,'
Simon's words when Alex went,
'that none of us is getting younger.
Time to let go, let young men take it on.
Old dogs should learn some new tricks
in what time that they have left.'

I think he found the new tricks that we practised
satisfying; if not, he'd missed his true vocation
and should have trod the Thespian boards.
It was as if he'd waited all his life to live.

Now hunger for experience assumed a dominance,
and all I offered he took eagerly.
Whatever I suggested he indulged.
I sold the businesses; we made the world our home.
In those four years we were our travel agent's joy.
Whatever strange exotic place came to his mind
became our destination.

Between, when constant travel frayed us,
some quiet weeks of sailing brought swift relief,
and home was Simon's yacht. I added now
another layer to the shaping of myself,
and stood apart at intervals to view in wonder
all the selves I had created
under guidance of these men.

A comfortable life — I thought with scorn
of those who saw it better to be

'young man's slave than old man's darling.'
Give me, I said, an old man any day.
There's little problem, then,
in having one's own way. But hazardous.
A danger that, or so it proved.
Against his wishes I had pressed for Santorini.
We moored, as always, in the shelter of the cliff.

The crater and its harbour swelled with craft;
Evenings brought sounds of revelry
from cliff face bars that echoed strains of music
from tourist ships below.
In such a night, when golden lights were twinkling
through the velvet black of night
that pooled below me in the crater,
I sat outside a small bar at the cliff top,
surveying all that loveliness.

The screeching crash of tearing wood and jagged masts
broke through the gaiety of dance band tunes,
all stilled with swift surprising speed
when it was heard the nightly ferry
had ploughed its devastation through a yacht.
Not someone's. Simon's.
I watched it all, a strange paralysis
that kept me seated
until they came to get me
to identify his body.

Still now, though it's ten years have passed,
I shiver when I live again that night.
He'd wanted so much
from the years that he had left –
he little knew how few they'd be.

The same dull feeling of resentment
fills me now, as then. I saw his body,
face unmarked

though bones were shattered where the mast
had caught him in its downward crash;
the etched look on his face of faint surprise
that all had come to this
will haunt me to my dying day.
Perhaps I did not love him,
but we'd made a life together
that was pleasing to us both.
And still I say: it was not fair.
His years of care for others
had merited a better recompense than this!

Perhaps I tried to blot it out.

You look at me enquiringly.
I'll swear, I had almost forgotten you are here.

Yes, blot it out. Three husbands dead –
one starts to wonder.
Old tales of jinxes, jonahs, surface in the mind.
But this, perhaps, is not surprising
when one's habitual choice is older men.
Maybe that helps explain
my next excursion into matrimony.

A younger man. It seemed a good idea.
No, this is not the truth.
That sounds a simple matter of a calculated choice.
But honesty compels me to admit
that it was more than this.
I'd vowed, way back, straight after Guy's desertion,
that never more would I allow a man
the power over me that he had had.

But now, forgetting caution, I ignored that vow,
and blundered into adolescent love.
Jed swore the difference in our ages did not matter,
that women of my years

had charms, maturity, that silly girls did not.
So eager! I sought only reasons to believe him.
Women in their forties are not old –
or so I told myself.
What's ten to fifteen years when passions rise?

I wonder now, in retrospect,
just when he marked me down,
potential prey, and set himself
the task of winning me.

No difficulty there – one comes to recognise,
expect shipboard romances, and I had my choice
of willing men. It pays to keep oneself in shape.
Flattering, as one day you will find,
to know oneself still able to attract, and see
the envious glances of the younger women
Jed by-passed for me. To feel again
that sense of being loved, desirable,
to wake each day in giddy knowledge
of a life that held excitement,
to feel each night the strength
of passionate young flesh,
the flooding of desire.
His body, hard and muscular,
his appetite insatiable – my breathing quickens
even at the memory of nights of passion with him.

The relish of the change from coaxing old men's penises
from dormancy into a feeble life,
for now I was the courted and desired.
Oh yes, I wanted him, and was prepared
like any silly foolish girl, love-sick,
to do whatever it was that he wanted.
Marriage? Reason told me everything
against it, but a madness still prevailed.

And yes, I am, as I have told you,
habituated to the married state.

Despite advice and sense,
I took my ardent cruise romance
into the world of everyday,
and Jed became my trophy man,
a testament to the eternal folly
of love-sickness that only ageing women feel.
My husband number four!

Re-definition yet again.
A new life, following his interests.
I learned about his world of sports cars,
races and casinos – of nights spent
at the roulette table waiting for
a blear-eyed dawn to draw us home to bed.
I could afford financial losses better
than the lack of sleep.
Insanity, of course! But not so dire
that remnants of a type
of prudence had deserted me.
The money still was mine,
an aspect he found disconcerting,
having estimated me an easier mark than this.
For so I'd seemed.

I do suspect a shadow of distaste has flickered
on your face. Not unlike that
on many of my friends', as I soon saw.
For folly runs its course, and I soon knew
what I had done.

A petulant young cub, who needed to be curbed,
at times whipped into shape.
I speak in metaphor, of course;
those days are over.

Though still I think with a fond smile
of poor fat funny Sol, who loved and needed me,
his chest of whips, cock rings and nipple pincers,
and wonder at the strangeness of the world.

Yet now I'm wandering from the point,
and really there is little more to tell.
Jed's challenges were brief;
a few smart flicks of the financial whip
and he was quick to come to heel.
His days of usefulness were past;
my brief excursion into folly over,
I saw that it was time for him to go.
It cost, but anything worth having
must be paid for, one way or another.
At least this one had ended as a discard,
not a corpse!

I had decided that the time had come
to try to find just who I was,
if buried deep beneath these layers
that had assumed so much protective coloration
through all the years of marriages,
there might still be a woman of her own.

Beneath the Ali, Alys, Lee, and Lissy,
all those personas that I have assumed,
is there a person who exists quite independent
of men who moulded me?
Who is Alicia? Is there anywhere a whole?

I'm boring you with this eternal speculation on my life.
This is my time for meditation,
for another question now confronts me.
You know I'm here with Francis;
this tour to Oberammergau was his decision,
not mine.

He chose to come again, as he has done before,
to see this passion play.

We fit together well; for years I've known him
as a genial host, a bon vivant, a man whose doors
are open to the world. What's new to me
is his attachment to his church – a world I've not
been part of, since my childhood days.
He's keen for us to marry,
and the way of life he offers is appealing.

We'd enter a secure and stable life;
I can well see a future with him.
Another layer in my self-creation?
I see myself returning to the church, and peace,
serenity, the marriage bed ahead once more,
a keeper of religious festivals, no Via Dolorosa,
perhaps the Stations of the Cross observed.

You note, I am acquiring yet another role.

But isn't this what life is all about?
A series of the roles we play?
What else should one expect?
Yet still I think,
in all this life, with all these men,
when have I ever been
the self I buried long ago?

Caroline

She's made me think.
She's made me wonder.
Not a cautionary tale, I know.

Yet too much there that struck
familiar notes.

Nights alone, wondering, Rob,
just where you are,
and who is lying in your arms.

The candles waiting for the match,
wine open, breathing,
as you've taught,
and then the waiting, waiting, waiting ...

Flowers next day are little compensation.

Too many clichés in my life.
Too many days I see the photos
on your desk, your children's smiling faces,
your arm around her shoulders.

Where am I in this?
Another trophy notched along your belt?

But then I think again –
the magic of your kiss,
the nights of passion we have shared,
the talk, the laughter, rightness
as I lie in your embrace.

Why should I think of her,
of them?

Abandon thought all you who enter here!

But I'm inside. And want to stay right here.

But not right here, right now
in Munich. We're moving on. The five,
my 'good old boys' have clearly had
a Munich beer or two while at their lunch
and now they're making happy tracks
towards the bus. Why are they here?

Pursed lips, a study in Teutonic disapproval,
Irmgard watches them climb up the steps.

BILL: THE GUILDSMAN'S TALE

Wel semed ech of hem a fair burgeys
To sitten in a yeldhalle on a deys.
Everich, for the wisdom that he can,
Was shaply for to been an alderman.

Each of them seemed a worthy burgess, fit to grace
A guild-hall with a seat upon the dais.
Their wisdom would have justified a plan
To make each one of them an alderman.

It's just that we've been mates
so many years – the only reason
that I'm here right now.
But Christ, it's not my cup of tea.
A bunch of nutters – that's what
I thought they'd be. Not sure
that I was wrong.

I look around, and ask myself
exactly how I came to be
roped in on such a trip.

The first weeks – easy to explain.
I'd always thought I'd like to travel
but Marge had never been too keen.
'You gotta see Australia first,'
that's what she used to say.

I tried to tell her we could leave
the Aussie travel for our latter years.
Join the grey nomads then, if that
was what she wanted.

We should do Europe first. But she
had lots of reasons to knock that.

She didn't want to fly. Had been up once
and got real airsick. 'Come off it,
Marge,' I said. 'That was a little plane.
You don't go overseas in one of those.'
No budging her. There never was.

So when I got the chance to join
my mates from work on what they called
a 'study tour' I jumped at it. Grinned
at the thought of us five blokes
let on the loose for study. But in fact
we worked much harder than
I'd ever thought. They kept us busy,
trotting round the foundries that
our bosses targeted. I was surprised
how much there was to learn.
Though, crikey, writing notes at night
was something of a downer.

I was a bit surprised how int'rested
I got at some of the new tricks
they were developing. The others
ate it up. Well, Mick and Len
have always had a liking for that sort
of stuff. Len started on the shop floor,
but put in lots of extra hours
on trying to find ways of doing jobs
more by machine. 'It's got to be
the coming world.' He used to spout this
any time he had a chance. 'You'll see,'
he told us often, 'it's automation.
That's the way the world will go.'

The rest of us would roll our eyes.
'Oh yeah, next thing we'll all be
without jobs – and thanks to you,
you fucking prick. You'll automate us
out of work.' He'd smile, but never
take offence. And work on late at night.

No surprise he got promoted.
More that we did too.
Works Manager, they call me now.
Done all right, the lot of us.
Never thought we'd make it into management.
We didn't put the hours in that Len did!

The one who took offence was Lenny's missus.
At work do's Raelene said it more than once.
'Not much use having someone who
comes home all hours and lies there
thinking of machines all night.'

It didn't take me long to cotton on
that there was meaning in her words.
I'm not too proud of what I did.
It wasn't all that often. Just a few
quick visits evenings when I knew
she'd be alone. I called it overtime
to Marge, made sure I worked
some extra nights to be convincing.

Always got a good reception from Raelene.
She sure gave me the old come-on,
but then I reckon all the others
got it too. I'm pretty sure they tried it on;
there was a time we found it hard
to look Len in the eye. Didn't think
he ever cottoned on that most of us
had shagged his missus once or twice.

But still I've never felt too good
about it. Mates are mates. You don't
let down a mate. And if she had
a wandering eye, we didn't have
to do the dirty on old Len.

It's funny, though she's gone –
she died a few years back –
when it came to the funeral,
just how bad we felt – the four of us.
Uncomfortable. After it was over,
Paddy said we ought to go to
Maid and Blackbird for a drink.

'Come on, Bill – least we can do now
for poor old Rae.' So he and Mick,
and Blue and I stood at that bar,
and drank a toast to her. But odd
the way we couldn't quite look at
each other as we downed the beer.
We never spoke of her again.

That's going back a bit. Almost
forgotten, yet every now and then
there's something brings it back to me.
Still don't feel good. You don't
do that to mates. Doesn't matter
if they know or not. Used to wonder
if Len had any idea what was going on.
Don't wonder so much any more.

So here we are, the five of us again,
this trip they sent us on, because
we've risen through the ranks, the lot of us,
and so the bosses thought we could
be useful for their future plans.

The free time at the end – that's bonus.
I was all for back to Paris. And Blue
was sure we could do well in Amsterdam.
He'd liked the look of girls
who waited for their customers in windows
down that street that all the tourists find.
Paddy thought we ought to do a quick trip
back to Ireland; he had addresses
his aging mum had given him.
He thought that Mick might be in that,
but Mick was talking Italy – bit of
a culture vulture is our Mick, and wanted to see
paintings, stuff like that. Quite a puzzle,
what to do. We knew we had to stick
together, but we all had different plans.

'So Len,' we said, 'you get to choose.
Which one?'

So far, he hadn't said a word. 'I want to go – '
He seemed to hesitate. No bloody wonder.
'There's one trip that I've always wanted.
To Oberammergau.' I guess he knew
we didn't have a clue. I'd never heard of it.

'Isn't that a churchy thing?' asked Mick.
He seemed to know a bit. 'Hadn't ever
figured you for one of them.'
Len just shook his head. 'Not any more.
But it's something that I've always
hoped to do. You said I get to choose.
Well, this is it.'

We didn't look too keen, I guess.

He told us more about the place, and how
the whole thing started. Didn't help.

OK. We'd given him the choice. But hell!
We hadn't planned on anything like this.

We all stayed quiet for a bit. We didn't want
to knock him back. But Paris … Amsterdam …
Even Ireland started to look good.

He waited for a while. 'Don't want to
pull rank here, but they were my machines
that got us on this trip. And then perhaps – '
he looked at us real straight – 'perhaps
you guys, my mates for many years,
may feel you owe me one.'

So here we are. And soon there's all this
church stuff that I guess we'll be in for
at Oberammergau. I think we all know
why we're here. It's not just Len's machines.
It's more that shaming feeling that
there's something that we need to pay for.

Can't go back and change the past,
but still I can't quite shake it off.
I've done the wrong thing by a mate.

Caroline

At last they're on the bus; I look around.
This surely should be time to talk,
but each seems settled in a private world.

I hesitate. Intrusion feels too crass.
Besides, the only vacant seat is that
beside our tour guide, Irmgard.
Even John's deserted me, and found a place
beside that mousy girl, the cooking contest winner.
I find myself annoyed. Irrational,
I know. I've made it clear
I'm not available, but still,
it's nice to feel pursued.
It looks as if my seat will be with Irmgard
Oh well, a chance to find a little more
from her perspective. She must see
many more, hundreds who come here
in never-ending cycles. Four performances
each week. They come, they see, they go.
A tidal pattern, ebb and flow,
six months, inexorable.

What does she know of them? I wonder.

Or is it just a job to her?

These people in their thousands, each three days.
What do they take away?
A travel story for the dinner table?
Or is there more?

That man, who gazes out the window,
not asleep, like most in post-lunch torpor.
A doctor, so John said. A specialist.
His gaze is fixed, abstracted.
What does he see? Or what not see?

GEOFFREY: THE DOCTOR'S TALE

With us ther was a Doctour of Phisyk,
In al this world ne was ther noon him lyk,
To speke of phisik and of surgerye ...

ᏆᎧ

A Doctor too emerged as we proceeded;
No one alive could talk as well as he did
On points of medicine and of surgery ...

The driver revs the engine;
the coach begins to move again.

I look around. Most others sleeping
through these sunlit southern German fields
with little picture postcard villages.
Soothing rhythm of the wheels.
I close my eyes again.

It helps to blot them out,
those figures who have stopped our progress.
Our driver had the decency to wait
until the last ones reached the other side.

We're well away from Munich now,
through Penzberg, Ohstadt, Eschenlohe,
along the Garmisch-Partenkirchen route.
I test the names, I savour them,
I roll them like a lozenge in my mouth.

Distract myself with words
in order to avoid the contemplation
of the ones I would ignore.
Those shambling figures being helped
across the road, the wheelchairs and the walkers.

But it's of little use. They have brought back the past.
Behind my lids I see the Matron watching me;
her gaze is careful, cautious.
She has to deal with many in this way.
I think back, flinching, to that last time
when I went to Rose.

'But doctor, I'm sure that you have seen this happen
many times before. I mean, a man who's worked
so many years in fields like yours would know
how common something like this is …'

Her smile was so benign, professional.
The Matron look, we'd called it back in days
when, caped and starched, those harridans
ruled wards and young probationers
stood quivering in corners.
'Matron's doing rounds.'
Even seasoned specialists could quail
when caught by Matron's minatory eye.
It's many years since I was faced by one
like that, but here again she was,
epitome of those lost arts,
ruling her decaying empire.

I've rarely seen the woman since the days
when Rose, poor Rose, first joined that world,
that twilight world
in which she's now a resident.

I'd have to say, at those first interviews,
the Matron seemed less prim,
much more the kindly friend,
the welcomer who understood our plight.

Though even then my wife had had her doubts.

'The rooms are lovely, true,
and all the staff we met'
(I note she didn't call them nurses)
'seem thoughtful and considerate ...
but Geoffrey, I'm not sure about that woman
at the interview. She smiled too much,
but only with her lips. Her eyes were hard.'

Yes, Rose – with all her limitations –
could voice perceptions
that would catch me unawares.

'Oh Geoff, it's such an institution,
but better than the others.
At least it doesn't have that smell.
There's nothing they can do
that will disguise the smell of age,
incontinence, stale food.
Try as they might.'

I must admit I was surprised.
Not just her frank appraisal
of the place, for it was accurate indeed,
but that she'd spoken of incontinence.
For Rose, a woman so fastidious, so puritanical
that love-making in daylight never had been possible,
preferred to leave the functions of the body
as a subject one should not discuss.

She viewed my work and life with, I suspect, revulsion.
I overheard her once, in conversation with a friend
who asked her how she coped with it ...

'With what?'

'It doesn't bother you? I wouldn't really want
my husband seeing other women naked all day long.'

Rose answered briefly, curt dismissal in her tone.
'I just don't think about it.
Look, he's a gynecologist.
Your husband's a psychiatrist ... what's worse?
Probing minds or bodies?
Besides, I think to Geoffrey
women are just specimens;
he might as well be in a lab.'

A little disconcerting how accurate she was.
In fact that brief assessment could have been
the story of my life. Perhaps our marriage too.
There's little to attract me in a woman's body
dealing with its intimacies all day long.

So Rose was wise to keep our coupling
always in the dark. Though when I think about it,
perhaps she'd understood my preferences ...

But if I'm truthful, as years went by,
there weren't too many beddings either.
I loved her and she knew it.
The lack of children seemed to leave us free
to function as companions, with affection.
I gave her a good life;
was never tempted to betray her.
I think we were the envy of our friends,
whose hazardous and often troubled marriages
brought nothing but distress.

What's made me think of all this now?
Now, when my whole objective
is to put it right away, forget
that vacant shambling figure
who was once my wife?

I wince still when I think of our last meeting;
a shudder of disgust runs through me.
Why think about it now?

If I'm honest I would have to say I know.

The coach had slowed.
Another little village on our route,
my fellow passengers, if not asleep,
yet in that hazy somnolence
after a good Germanic lunch en route,
our driver mercifully quiet for a change,
relentless tour guide spiel abandoned
lest he disturb post-prandial naps.
I glanced indifferently at bell towers
on scattered local churches,
crowning white-washed walls
in this weak summer sun.
Must be a hospital, or home, I'd mused,
when our bus gradually slowed, and stopped.

A sad procession so laboriously trailed its way
across the road. Wheelchairs pushed by girls
in bright blue uniforms, while others helped the hunched
and bent, who placed their canes with trembling care
before each step was tentatively tried.
Their vacant eyes gazed blankly at our bus;
we're creatures from another planet.

We are indeed. For in our group we're fighting off
that moment that we know will come, the day
when the relentless march of time will catch us too.

Not that, I think. Dear God, if you exist,
preserve me from the losses,
the humiliations of old age.
Let me die decently, with all my wits about me.

And that, I know, is why my thoughts are back with Rose.

I'm back in years of waiting rooms, knowing well
the outcome they will gently, pityingly,
bring to our attention. Or sitting there beside her,
willing her reluctant mind to call back details
of the names she should remember.

White-coated figures study her with sympathy,
and ask their questions with grave courtesy.
'Rose, do you know the date today?
Who is Prime Minister?
I want you carefully to listen to three words I'll say.
Remember them. A little later on
I'll ask you what they were.'

The panic in her eyes,
aware that she can answer nothing,
can perform no tasks.
'Count backwards from 100.'

She brightens briefly, thinking this might be achieved.
But then the doctor adds, 'Count back by sevens.'
We all know this is way beyond what she can do.

Yet still through all those early days
and tests, she'd hoped. Her tremulous apology.
'I've never had a head for figures.'

'Can you recall the three words that I asked you
to remember?'

Blind misery,
for they have gone,
and simple words,
like 'clock, tree, painting'
are obliterated.

A charted course ahead, as now we study carefully
their diagrams that show the parts of brain that still
are vivid on the page. And know how fast
they will diminish. PET scans and MRIs give
little comfort, when the pictures they reveal
are bleak and presage only gloom.

I wonder if, in some dim afterworld,
Alois Alzheimer can hear the knell of doom
that invocation of his name
has rung in many failing minds.

Not only theirs, but in the minds of those who love
and care for them. For it is not the mind alone,
capacity for logic, memory, thought,
that slowly, bit by bit, erodes, diminishes
and ultimately disappears,
but all that made the person who she was.

'You must,' they warned us, 'realise that
many other things will also go. The attributes
and qualities that are your personality,
these too may change.'

They tried hard to prepare us
for mood swings, for aggression, failing memory,
language breakdown. We knew the road
to darkness was ahead,
and that the losses would be grievous.

'What will become of me?' she cried.

A sort of blind bewildered misery
would surface in her eyes.
I saw her grope for words
that now eluded her,
slipping from her grasp like fish
who slithered back into the sea of language

she could no longer angle in.
I watched with pain the slow inexorable march
that saw her lose herself,
become a sad distortion of the woman she had been.

But still we could rejoice in thinking of past times,
for episodic memory lasted, and while recall
of yesterday had gone, the holiday we took
at least two decades back was still as clear as day.

We talked so much of Oberammergau, our days
in that small place, a time we were at peace
and happy with each other. We'd walked the streets
and watched the people, marvelled at the postman
on his bike, for earlier in that day we'd seen him
as the Caiaphas who urged the crucifixion on the Jews.

Her memory for these small details, sharp,
unclouded for the moment.
'Remember in the shop?
The girl who played the Virgin Mary sold us
Christmas decorations that same night?'
I marvelled.

I'd forgotten, but to her it was still clear as yesterday.
Or clearer.
Yesterday had gone, but twenty years ago
was vivid in that fading mind.
'Oh Geoffrey, I'd so love to do that trip again.
I know I can't. But do it for me, please.
And think about the fact
that we were happy there, a while.'

Implicit memory lasted also,
so for a time the actions that make up
the trivial patterns of each day were easy to perform.
We knew these too would go.

Then all the simple routines daily life requires
would soon become incomprehensible. A toothbrush
would become an object of concern, dismay.

But not, dear God, not yet. We wanted only
to preserve what still could be retained.

She tried. We tried.
We followed the research with infinite care,
and every faint and flickering hope
of bringing if not cure at least a way to slow its progress
gave us a brief if fleeting joy. We studied diets,
exercised, tried yoga, meditation,
practiced frequent mind games, did the crosswords
in each daily paper, such assiduous mental work.

Canute had never tried so hard to keep the sea at bay.

So then more anguish as I watched her mind
move down the faltering path that had been set for it.
The shutters lowered and the lights of reason dimmed.

We'd looked ahead, and known. She had decided it.
'I don't want you to care for me. You still have life,
your work. Besides, your ladies do adore you.
What would they do, without you there to steer them
through all those female miseries they face?'

I checked her face for mockery, but it was bland.
'We'll find a place. You'll scarcely notice that I've gone.
It's better so.'
I knew that she was right.

Somehow she sensed when it was time,
and in the flashes of spasmodic understanding
that were now so rare she asked to go.

I left her there, bewildered, in the place
we had selected. I drove away, uncertain
whether she, the figure seated on the bed,
or I looked more forlorn at parting.
And yet I wondered as I left.

Too soon?
For still the changes they'd forewarned
had not occurred.
Brief flashes, yes, of anger,
and moments of despair.
But she remained as always,
calm, still, careful of herself.
The Rose of old.

I sometimes think,
if she had stayed with me,
perhaps the wife I knew
might yet have been preserved.
For now, enduring all these months of solitude,
I've seen the tide encroaching on the sand,
a steady loss, a diminution and reduction.
She is no longer Rose.

'The lights are on, but no one's home.'

The first time that I read these words, I shuddered;
their truth was horrible to me.
But now I understand that it is better so,
for bit by bit a woman
whom I do not recognise has surfaced.
And this is what the Matron tries
to draw to my attention.
In spite of all her careful tact and delicacy,
I know what she is telling me is true.

'But doctor, I'm sure you have seen this happen
many times before. I mean, a man who's worked
so many years in fields like yours would know
how common something like this is ...
We see it frequently. All inhibitions go ...

Because my field is women, she assumes I understand
the workings of their minds. What does she think?
Perhaps that they would tell me of their dreams,
their deep desires? Is this what lies inside all women?

I cannot see Rose any more. It hurts.
It is too shaming, too distressing.

That she, always so modest, careful,
even prudish, should now make such an exhibition
of herself. She cannot now be left with any man,
and staff have trouble keeping clothes on her.
all sense of decency is gone,
a creature of lewd appetites has taken over this,
the body of my wife. It seems as if
whatever were the innermost controls
that kept her modest, chaste,
have now been thrown aside
to leave free rein for someone I have never seen.

The last time that I spent with her has left me sickened.

My memories of former years are tarnished now.
And the inevitable question. Always now the question.

For is this what she always was? Was our marriage
just a sham, a product of dissembling?

So now, if I examine years together,
I know that, in the days when we still shared a bed,
it was my voice that said 'Turn out the light.'

If I remove the comfort of the memories I've created,
it's time to see the many nights
she moved to me, enquiring,
her soft hand tentatively on my thigh,
only to find me turning from her,
curt, rebuffing.

'Not tonight. Tomorrow's a big day.
Let's just sleep.'

Those nights I could obliterate,
ignore the faint half-stifled sigh she breathed,
a recognition of frustration for the night to come.

And so it's not uncommon, Matron?
You find yourself a watchdog over many such?
We must ask then
how many husbands did not recognise the needs
they were not meeting. An irony indeed,
that I, whose work is women and their bodies,
so failed the one
I should have understood the best.

I look around me, see the sleepers on this bus.
Who knows the secrets of their minds,
the passions, unacknowledged buried thoughts,
desires, vague yearnings they refuse to bring into the light,
for fear of judgement by the ones they love?

It may not be uncommon,
but it's a mockery for me of all the years
we shared. I cannot bring myself
to look upon this travesty
of someone I have loved.
For now it's just disgust I feel.
I cannot watch this wreckage of our lives.
I will not visit her again.

I stare determinedly beyond these scenes,
and as our coach nears Oberammergau
I see again those signs that so excited us last time this way.
Our little rental car, Rose poring over maps
and carefully articulating multi-syllables
of unfamiliar names.
'We must be close.
I see a sign to Unterammergau.
It can't be far from here.'

Excitement almost palpable. Our first real holiday
for many years. A time when in this place
we found again a pleasure in each other
attrition of our daily lives had quite eroded.

For her it had a greater meaning,
more than I could comprehend, but for us both
it was a brief renewal. All too brief.

Back home we slipped again into familiar patterns.
Sometimes I fancied that she looked at me with puzzled eyes,
as if she did not understand what life had brought.

What was she thinking then?

My only hope is to obliterate what I now know,
and live again the past.
If I can in this little German town
recapture what we had,
find here the Rose of former times,
I may be able to recall the woman I once loved,
and find it in my heart to quell disgust
and love her still.

Caroline

Lots of oohs and aahs, and 'look at thats'
as we drive into Oberammergau. We passed
through Unterammergau, anticipation rising
in the bus, and soon the craggy peak
of the Zugspitze was behind, and everyone
awake, alert. We now see painted houses,
pictured fairy tales, with every wall
a new delight. Irmgard sits back,
and preens herself as if each mural has been
her own work. How many tourist buses
does she guide each month? I wonder.

The bus stops, and there's general approbation.
The hotel's small, but charming,
with window boxes spilling festooned flowers
down the walls. High gables give a story book
look to the roof, and even blasé travellers
voice their pleasure.

Through Garten Café to Reception they all troop,
to find their keys and rooms.
I watch them mount the stairs.
'No elevator?' murmurs Alison, but Francis,
ever gallant, takes her arm.

Last to be taken up above are that strange pair,
the woman – Russian? Czech? Hungarian? –
who seems to be with Alexander Newman,
a name I've seen my paper feature often lately.
But yet they're not a couple, more like
slightly wary friends. A story there, I think,
though doubtful that I'll hear it.
A very private pair.

ALEXANDER:
THE MERCHANT'S TALE

This worthy man ful wel his wit bisette
Ther wiste no wight that he was in dette,
So estatly was he of his governaunce
With his bargaynes, and with his chevisaunce

This estimable Merchant so had set
His wits to work, none knew he was in debt,
He was so stately in negotiation,
Loan, bargain, and commercial obligation.

Still raining – but at least the place looks good.
The rooms are comfortable, bed feels soft.
The blonde-haired pigtailed girl who brought us up
took Svetla to the room next door,
then with a smile showed me how mine also
gave views across the town
and to the Zugspitze,
piercing the valley's misty afternoon.

'So you have *Mittagessen* taken?' she asked earnestly.

'We ate in Munich,' I assured her hastily.
Another heavy German meal would finish me, right now.

'Then *Abendessen* will be served tonight;
a bell will ring to tell you.

I nodded, and she left. My cases were already waiting;
the bed looked so inviting. Damn nuisance
I'd agreed to take the optional excursion
our guide had recommended highly for the hours
still left to us this afternoon.

But Svetla had seemed keen;
this whole trip's more her show than mine.

I shake my head in wonder that I'm sitting here right now
in this small southern German town. How come?
I ask myself. All very well – good move, in fact –
to get away from home right now. The situation
had become a little hot, I would admit.

Not something I'd say to the others,
but phone calls (how the hell did they get hold
of what I was assured would be a silent number!)
and floods of emails (easily deleted, that's quite true)
were bad enough.

The final crunch came, though, when little posses
started to stake out my house.
I moved, of course,
and found myself a brand-new penthouse, river views.

But nothing stopped them. Still a few hung on,
even collared a reporter and a camera man.
The photo next day in the morning paper
could not have been less flattering.

I'll swear I really looked as if I might have been
the man the article made out.
I asked my old mate Ted –
he's been the one who's kept me on the right side
of the law (though only just) for many years –
if we could sue for slander.

Well, libel, as he pointed out, and no,
they'd put it very carefully. 'Nothing there,'
he said regretfully. 'They've been quite cautious
in the things they said, old son.
There's nothing you can get them on.

A pity, though. You don't exactly
come out smelling clean.
Not what they say, though;
it's all there between the lines.
I'd keep my head down for a while, if I were you.
Perhaps some time away?
Might be a good idea to take a trip somewhere?'

A canny bloke, old Ted.
We go way back together, back to school.
Those days he always saw a way
of keeping his nose clean. We sometimes touched
the edges of the rules, but he could always talk us
out of trouble, even then.

I still remember how my dad,
another shrewd old bird, once said to me,
'That friend of yours, that Edward,
I'll swear the bugger can make
black seem white – and not just white,
but lily pure at that!'

This last affair of mine had really put Ted to the test.
Nothing shady. Just a little grey around the margins.

It could have made them all a lot of money,
if the market hadn't sunk at the worst time.
It's not my fault if all those greedy people lost their shirts.

OK. The mum-and-dad investors
that the papers got so hot about –
I will admit for them it was a pity.
They knew, they should have known,
that any deal that offered gains like mine must be a risk.

That's not illegal, is it!
It offered big big profits, as I said.
Not my responsibility.

I'm not my brother's keeper.
No way I could have known how bad the crash would be.
The fact that I was bright enough to get my money out
in time just showed good business sense.
And if some of the money-shifting takes us
into murky waters, again
that's just another part of risk in all these things.

They're paying for my expertise, that's all.
It's only fair I should be recompensed.
As my dad used to say – he said it many times:
'In this world, boy, a man must look
after himself; there's no one else will do it for you!'

In spite of this, I didn't relish it that day
they printed photos of my home and cars.
A man has every right to spend
his money as he chooses.
So Ted's advice to cool it, get away,
wait till it all blew over made good sense.

The last eight weeks I've come to wonder
if there's more to life than wheeling, dealing,
watching markets every day.
I dropped a bit in London at the gambling clubs,
but then I could afford it.

A few good nights in Paris, but my main plan
was to find the places that my old Dad told me of.

He never liked to talk much of his past;
in fact it's true he quite clammed up when asked.
For many years I didn't even know
we should have had a different name,
or that my dad, the man I'd always known as Newman,
John Newman, was on arrival, back in 1951,
called Jiri, Jiri Novotny, a name, he once admitted,
that he'd changed before he married Mum.

A not uncommon thing to do,
and one he felt was fitting.
For *Novotny* meant a 'new man';
this was the name he chose.
He smiled, an odd look on his face,
'I needed to be new, so new man
was good name to take.'

He wouldn't tell me more, not then.
I thought, well, fair enough.
He'd come to a new land, new start, and this new name.
It seemed appropriate. I let the matter drop.
These days I have a different picture of it all,
of all the past.

I had to try to piece together bits that he let slip.
I'd found he came from parts of Europe new to me,
these days the Czech Republic, but back then,
Czechoslovakia.

He wouldn't tell me much.

The years of World War 2, he fought, I gathered,
but not in an army. It seemed to me
it must have been the underground, the Resistance,
those men who bravely undermined
the German occupation of their land.

Not quite my style, to put my life at risk …
but still I felt a sort of pride, a hero for a dad,
even if he wouldn't talk about it.

'Let be,' my mum advised.
'He doesn't like to think about those times.'

These days I understand it better,
why he blotted out the memories.

He never had too much to say,
not just to us, but anyone at all.
Just concentrated on the business,
made it clear that this was what a man
was measured by.

Not easy being son to such a man.
We never kicked a footie round,
or went on camping trips.
His life was solitary;
couldn't blame my mum for taking off.
At least she waited till I'd finished,
graduated, got myself set up with that first firm.

I sometimes wondered what his pleasures were;
no friends – he wouldn't join the Czech Club –
no hobbies, sports. His whole life was the factory.
No wonder it did well.

Even there he seemed to take no pleasure
in the crafting of the furniture they made,
but only in the profits. 'Make money, boy!'
His words ring in my ears.
That faintly twisted English that he spoke.
'We have no other language in this house!'

He threw away the past with his old name.
He was indeed the 'new man' that he wanted.

So any childish questions that I asked
met only curt rebuffs. We got on better
when I started to do well.
He watched me wheel and deal
with faint approving nods.

'There's nothing else you can depend on, boy.
Make money; that's what life is all about.
Forget the rest, the bullshit that they talk.'

But just before he died he let it slip.
He still had family over there.
I might have uncles, cousins, I had never known.
He told me where, in Prague, his home had been.

It seemed a good idea,
when I took on this exile, to go there.
A hunt for family, you could call it.
Besides, I was intrigued.
I'd always wanted to know more.
This man, resistance fighter,
rejecting all his past, cutting every tie,
re-making this whole life –
I wanted to know more
about the stock that I came from.

Surprise to me, how easily I found them.
That old address was still a starting point,
though now to my surprise
it was a home for aged, infirm.
A grand old home,
it seemed to me a pity to see it so abandoned.

I asked for the Director;
her name, black-lettered on the office door:
Novotny.

And so I met my cousin Svetla,
imposing in her tailored suit, sleek hair,
her English fluent (big relief at that!),
her manner business-like, professional.
I'm usually good at meeting people;
situations rarely phase me.
I introduced myself with confidence.

'You are my uncle Jiri's son?'
It wasn't quite the greeting I'd expected. Her face …

almost a look of faint distaste.
Where was the warm reunion I'd anticipated?

'Your card said 'Newman' was your name?'

I found myself defensive;
her tone was cautious, hostile even.
'My father changed his name
when he came to Australia.'

'That I can understand. Why have you come?'

It seemed a challenge, and I stumbled
through explanations of my father's death,
a wish to find my family, my travels,
but all without the normal ease.
'This is the family home?' I asked at last.

She sighed. 'How much do you know of the past?'

'Almost nothing.' It was true.

'So come to dine with me tonight, and we will talk.
Come here at eight. I live in rooms above.
Now I must go; I have elsewhere appointment.'
Her nod was curt, dismissive.

Well, that went well! I thought resentfully,
as through the afternoon I wandered
round Prague's streets alone. Across the cobbled stones
of Republiky Square, past the black Powder Tower,
down mazes of small Old Town streets
through milling crowds who jostled, waiting for
the hourly chimes from that famed Astrological Clock.

I yawned. Another one parading figures
portraying every vice, and finally the rooster crow,
betrayal's classic signal.

It struck no sense of home to me, this place.
Yet this is where my roots have been,
these streets my father must have walked
each day.

Obligatory, the hotel's brochure made it clear,
a visit to St Vitus', the cathedral with its tomb
of sainted Wenceslas.
Back home each schoolchild
knew the song, and rarely passed
a Christmas without *Good King Wenceslas*.

The hours were passing, and I checked my guide again.
The Jewish Cemetery?
It would be too late; in any case
it was of little interest to me.
The dead are dead.

At eight, equipped with wine and flowers,
I pressed the bell outside the wooden entrance gates,
odd apprehension in my bones. Absurd.
She seems formidable, I thought,
but just a cousin, after all.

Her welcome was a little warmer,
her gravity more understandable.

'A month before this and you would have met my brother,
Miroslav. He died, God rest his soul.'
She crossed herself.

The meal was good. We talked of casual things.
My mother, and my father's work, the timber business
that had raised him from a penniless newcomer
to a substantial man of property.

I glanced up from my goulash soup
and caught her look
before she masked it.
'Yes, property has always been important in our family.'

'This house is quite magnificent;
how have you kept it all these years?'

'It now belongs no longer to us, but the state.
But then, it never really should have been our property.'

I looked my question.
'No, let us eat now and enjoy the meal.
Later, over coffee, I will answer all your questions.'

She rose, and went to serve the pork and dumplings.
We talked of other things.

Now, looking back upon that evening,
I can relive the lack of comprehension,
stunned disbelief, the sense of outrage.
Then, at last, the growing horror
as I listened to her story.
Resistance fighters? No!

For Jiri and his brother Vlad were none of those.

Instead, they'd seen the war through other eyes;
the chances that it gave them. How much did they believe
the anti-Jewish rubbish that they spouted?
Were they true anti-Semites,
or did they see an opportunity too good to miss?

'This house,' she said, her gesture infinitely sad,
'back then it was the home of Mandelbaums.
Their firm was prosperous;
your father and mine also worked for them.

You will not know about this, but when this land came
under German rule, and we were part of the Protectorate,
in 1939 all Jewish businesses were vulnerable;
a firm with any Jew involved could then be 'Aryanised.'
You understand this term?'

I nodded, still confused.

'The Mandelbaums were good men, brothers too.
They saw what future lay ahead for them;
in simple trust they put these two young men,
my father and your father, in control,
believing when this time of madness ended,
they could resume their role.

They did not foresee or understand
the fascists in our midst.
They did not know that they would,
like so many others, be betrayed.

For these two men, my uncle and my father,
saw their chance to gain the business and the house.
I doubt they hesitated.
Instead, denounced their friends, who had so trusted them.
Like others – there many Czech fascists –
they vied to share the spoils
that came with yellow stars,
and soon the Mandelbaums and thousands more
were on the road to deportation.
No matter.
Our family had the house as well as business.'

'But the resistance fighting?'
I hardly could accept her words.

Svetla's laugh was harsh. 'Was that his story to you?'

In thinking back I felt uncertain.
Had this indeed been based on words he spoke,
or on my wish to see my father as a hero?

She saw my deep unease,
her voice was gentler now.
'This has been hard for you to hear.
You need some time to think.
Come back tomorrow, and we go to Terezin.
There you may come to understand.'
We parted silently.

We didn't speak much on the drive to Terezin,
that ancient fortress that had always been a prison.
She gave me facts and figures;
the more than 30,000, mainly Jews,
who passed that way en route to other prisons
or death camps of the Nazis.

I look back on that day at Terezin and try to blot it out.

The nightmare of the Small Fortress,
the vicious irony above the gate,
where scrolled *Arbeit macht frei*
still greets the visitor.
We saw the way the town became a Jewish ghetto,
except that execution grounds
and mass graves were new features.
Here, in these cells,
some housing fifty, sixty, ninety prisoners,
I knew the Mandelbaums had lived.
Yet still the Jewish leaders
tried brave attempts at order and normality.
In the museum most poignant relic of the time,
the children's drawings ...

'It was not just the Mandelbaums who died.'
Her commentary as we drove past the complex,

that vast cemetery, continued tonelessly,
quite matter-of-fact.
'The brothers were responsible for many
who were then denounced, betrayed.
They did extremely well from it,
until the liberation came.'

'Was there no reckoning for them?'

'For my father, yes. Resistance fighters
acted fast. There was no mercy
for those who had committed such betrayals.
They came for him one night.
We did not find his body.
Our mother did not wait; she killed herself.
Your father saw his fate and fled in time.
He was the younger brother.

Did he indeed escape?'

I pondered, could not answer.
I thought of that sad lonely man,
who sat each night with only ledger sheets
and loss and profit statements as his friends.

'How can I tell?
Does anyone escape what they have done?

And what of you?'

'I and my brother felt always the need
to make a reparation.
The state now owns the house;
the Communists have seen to that,
but we have worked here all these years.
In caring for these people
we may blot out some guilt.
It is, perhaps, atonement.

We spend our lives in seeking pardon for all
our family has done. And each ten years
we visit Oberammergau. To ask forgiveness.
We planned, again this year, to see the Passion Play –
you know it? But now my brother will not be with me.'

I wonder if in any way
I could have said no to her plea;
that I should take her brother's place on this,
their journey of atonement.
She made it clear that in her eyes
I too shared in my father's guilt.
He ran, escaped due retribution.

I am indeed my father's son.

I turn back inwards from the window,
but not before I see the clouds that shroud
the Zugspitze. They form, and swirl,
and form again. It almost seems
that there are faces in them.
Despairing Jewish faces,
old men and haggard women,
the children who have lost their futures.
My father's guilt hangs heavy on me.

But there among the swirling clouds
I also fear to see the other faces,
faces I can recognise.
They turn towards me bleak
with imprecations and despair.
In silent misery they look at me
accusingly.

It's harder now to turn away from them.

Caroline

The Wies – they call it. Eighteeenth century,
she said, and always known to be
a church for pilgrimage. Appropriate.
I'm coming more and more
to feel that's what we are.

Oval, rococo, most elaborate in its style.
World Heritage, she tells us.
The tour is optional, but it's made quite clear:
one not to miss.

We're sold. Most of our group will go.
Rob, this would be so good
if you were here to share it with me.
It's what I want, I long for,
lives that we could share.

Instead, I'll be with John, the actor
whom I've mentioned. He's witty,
cynical, perceptive. Fun to talk to.
An attractive man – three wives
are testimony there. But he's not you.

I want you with me. Ache with longing.
Want to tell you what I'm doing,
to describe these people to you.

But fear. What if our time together
has come to an end?
I am afraid.

JETHRO: THE PARDONER'S TALE

But trewely to tellen, ate laste,
He was in chirche a noble ecclesiaste.
Wel coude he rede a lessoun or a storie,
But alderbest he song an offertorie;
For wel he wiste, whan that song was songe,
He moste preche, and wel affyle his tonge,
To winne silver, as he ful wel coude.

But still to do him justice, first and last,
In church he was a noble ecclesiast.
How well he read a lesson or told a story!
But best of all he sang an Offertory,
For well he knew that when that song was sung
He'd have to preach and tune his honey-tongue
And (well he could) win silver from the crowd.

Dear brothers and sisters, my dearly beloved
sisters and brothers, are you lonely, are you distressed?
Tonight I bring you a message of joy and love.
You need never feel alone again. Just hear my words,
allow yourselves to sink into the peace I bring.

It's the standard opening to my show. And then
the music swells. I know my words will go
to all those thousands who are watching,
who yearn for what I have to tell them.
I meet their need.

They brought us here by coach. A smaller bus this time.
An afternoon to fill, before tomorrow's Passion Play.
The tour guide talked it up, this jaunt to Wies.

'You won't regret the time – it's just an hour away.
A very special church, the Wies.'
I guess she gets commission.

Not everyone has chosen this side trip.
I'm still unsure just why I'm here, I'd have to say.
The woman, the nosy one on board the bus,
asked me that question.

Hardly my type, I like them softer, feminine.
This one well-dressed and groomed,
professional, I'd guess,
that polished hard-faced look they get,
alert and curious. She's sure inquisitive.
I've watched her since we left.
She gets around. She chats us up,
and always with an air of someone
docketing away our details, noting what we say.

I know that look.
I've felt it on my own face
as I work my way through crowds in gatherings.
I'm gaining information, taking mental notes
to be examined, mined for useful details
after they have gone.
I wonder what her game is.
Thought at first she might be on the make,
looking for a new fish she could hook.
Now I'm not so sure,
there's something else she's after.

'You're interested in churches?' her opening gambit
when she gestured to the empty seat beside her.

I nodded non-committally. I'm sure she knows
exactly who I am. My public's quite extensive,
and weekly ratings on my show ensure that even

in Australia, where she comes from,
few viewers wouldn't know my name.
Though there, they tell me,
preachers with a show like mine
are only given air time in small hours of the night.

No problem there,
for that's when viewers are most vulnerable;
my best response comes from the lonely, friendless,
the unhappy ones. They need my message.
They will hear.
But it's the major channels – those who give me
prime time viewing spots –
it's there where reputations
rise or fall.

'And this one's something special,'
she goes on. 'The guide books say it ranks
among the most outstanding samples of baroque.'

Again I nod, then turn the question back to her,
a technique that I've practised many years.
'And you?
Is this a special interest that you have?'

'Let's say,' she answers smoothly, 'my interest
lies more in its origins, the story of its building.
After all, it's pulled the masses in for centuries.'

I glanced at her quite sharply then,
to look for subtleties,
but there was nothing in her face,
no knowing look, no hint of hidden barb
or covert criticism of my work.
I even wondered if perhaps she did not realise
that pulling in the masses with religious bait
was just where I excelled.

But then,
there's precedent for what I do.
A great command indeed. So I too fish for men.

We talked of architecture, great cathedrals
we had seen, of rival claims of Gothic, Romanesque,
of how baroque in Portugal had found an extreme form
till Manueline's wedding cake extravagances
could leave the viewer breathless –
but left unanswered her implicit question:
why was I, a preacher from tent ministries,
from radio and TV screens,
a man who, in the States, is known
from coast to coast,
inspecting buildings of the past,
the relics of an age when faith was certain,
anchored more in art and architecture –
stained glass windows, bricks and mortar?

And if she'd pressed the question,
what might then my answer be?

I wondered if she'd read reports of Senate hearings,
the way the dealings of my ministry had been examined,
the careful articles in newspapers and magazines
that stopped just short of being actionable.

'No,' said my lawyers quite regretfully,
'there's nothing there that we can sue.
It's all been scrutinised; it stops just short of libel.
Well-gauged.'
With what I pay them I'd expected more than this,
and not their cautious pussy-foot advice
I might be wise to lie low for a bit,
or find some new approach.

'Do something different,' they advised.
All very well, but what?
It wasn't till my PA found this trip, this tour
to Oberammergau, that pennies dropped.

At first I couldn't see the point, but she's a canny lass
so very soon I saw where she was heading ...
She's right. There's good potential here
to re-establish my credentials.

'And not,' she was insistent, 'just another of your tours,
first class, gold-plated, 5 star beds the whole way round.
You go like all the rest, an ordinary man. That's where
the market value's going to be.

She's young, is Bridget, but she knows the world.
I value her advice. 'You never know,'
her tone was silky,
'You may surprise yourself. Perhaps you'll have ...'
I laughed – it was our standard joke –
we chimed the words together:
'... an epiphany!'

That woman seated near me had quite a look
of Bridget. I reckon she too knows
just what is what.
We chatted on, but I was wary.
There was more behind her comments,
I was sure. Too many questions!
beware a woman who asks questions.

Relief came with arrival at the church.
I lost myself among the other tourists flocking in
to this, a tourist Mecca, one may say! I smiled.

In jostling crowds, we passed the stalls
of souvenirs, of holy water, cards and trinkets.
I looked approvingly.

They know the way to make a buck.

We in the trade get good at spotting opportunities,
and here they had the tourist game sewn up.
The credulous were spending well.

We passed the little chapel
where all this story started.
That building's days were numbered
when pilgrim flocks began to come to Wies in droves.

A more impressive home was needed for the statue.
Now beyond us lay, against the backdrop of the mountains,
the wedding cake construction, white and gold,
that we had come to see.
Too fancy for my taste by half,
but when a sudden unexpected shaft of sun
broke through the grey of afternoon
it had a moment's look that took me
back to childhood and those pictures in my parents' book.
Heaven's streets all paved with gold. Yes, well ...

Funny, I hardly ever think of them.
But when I do I know how much I owe them.
Street preachers, both of them.
Many afternoons my job to take around
the tin and ask donations from the listeners.
Got quite good at spotting just which women
would be moved to give to boys like me,
skinny and deprived, with earnest pleading eyes.
Oh yes, I earned my keep.
watched and learned, and then,
when I was old enough,
they let me give my testimony.

I was lucky. Had the voice,
never went through acned years.

They'd taught me well.
I knew the stories that would get
the listeners in, and quoted scripture soon as well
as mum and dad. I guess the difference was that
they believed what they were saying.
To me it was a living. I knew that I could reach
a bigger audience than ever they had dreamed of.

They didn't understand the possibilities;
they didn't feel the lure of power.
Crowds hanging on your words,
eating from your hands.

They were disturbed the night I told them
I had changed my name.
'We called you Ebenezer' – that was mum,
all earnest – 'for what it means.
You were to be a stone of help,
like Samuel's in the Bible.'

I didn't see myself on radio,
(already my ambition) as Ebenezer Jones.
The new name chosen mollified their doubts a little.

'Well son,' Dad's voice was dubious,
'at least Jethro is Biblical.
He's father-in-law to Moses.'

I'd have to say that Jethro Jones has proved
a good name for TV. Sounds sort of catchy,
honest even. Good for the image.

But mum and dad, for all their zeal,
were not the ones who got me into radio –
that was Dean Huber, (famous name back then;
I doubt that many know of him today)
who came to me one afternoon.

He'd heard me in the street and said that
he could use me for a spot.
He had a nightly show back then, and thought
a voice of youth would add
a new drawcard to his appeal.
He little foresaw that, with his star waning,
mine would rise. I still recall his words
the day the network dropped him,
the day he found his program now was mine.
'God is not mocked, my boy.
Your day will come.'

I wondered at the Senate hearing whether the old man
was right. Maybe my day had come?

But good accountants covered my affairs so well,
and while I paid the earth for fancy lawyers
they were worth their price.
I came out smelling not too bad,
if not exactly roses, not like sewage either.
Advice they gave was sound.
'Cooperate!'
I did, with limitations.
But not outright refusals, like Copelands and the Whites.
As for Creflo Dollar and Bishop Eddie Long –
it's attitudes like theirs that make us all look bad.
But then, just like the Bakkers,
they'll live on to fight – and preach –
another day, because the message that we give
is what our people want.
God promises his people will do well.

A simple message . The label that they gave it
isn't wrong.
'Prosperity!' they trumpet as an accusation.
True! We preach it.
So it's a gospel of prosperity.

There's nothing wrong with that.
If we, their leaders, can embody it,
it gives a confidence
to what we promise for our followers.

'Televangelists' our critics call us.
But I'm not ashamed. It's my calling;
it's my job. My people know me,
and they hear my voice.
(I know you'll criticise me quoting that!
Another one, although he lacked the benefit of media,
was not ashamed to make that claim. And nor am I!)

My brothers and my sisters, if good things
happen to you, the world outside will judge you.
You get a big new house;
a person who lacks one
will always criticise and judge.
I know. I have been judged by those
who do not understand.
Paul said: 'I don't care what you think of me.'
Like him, we have no need to care
what others think of us.
Paul said: 'It is the Lord himself who judges me!'
And to his faithful, he will give good things.
Just wait, and your reward will come.
You can be sure of this.
Dear friends, do not lose heart.
Face troubles bravely.
For we are told, nay, we are promised,
that blessings will be poured upon the faithful.
So persevere!
I tell you, you will prosper.

Now take the church we're looking at. The Wies.
It's almost like a model for the argument I'm making.
Stunning, sure.

No wonder that it's listed as World Heritage;
UNESCO knows what it's about,
and even though it's set way out here
in the countryside, in fields of crops
and grazing animals, it sure pulls in the masses.

Thousands of pilgrims every year –
and that's beside the tourist crowds,
who come exclaiming loudly
at this crazed elaboration
– OK, rococo splendour –
that we see.
The swirls of stone, the carvings, gold
everywhere, and all against the lightness of white walls
and wild extravagance of murals.

That ceiling! You stand, gaze upward,
transfixed by scene on scene of angels,
mounted horsemen, battles, cross aloft.
Eyes wander down, and marvel at the intricate,
the stonework that they see
in pulpit, lectern, baptistry, until they fix at last
upon the wooden figure of the Saviour Scourged,
whose tears gave Wies its fame.

A fascinating tale, indeed, and one that
proves my point. The masses need
their promises and miracles.

If, way way back, those two deluded peasants
had not been moved to pity for a statue
cast out from processions,
too grim and gruesome to be carried with the others,
and given it a refuge in their farmhouse in the Wies,
this church would not exist,
and I would not be here.

So chance rules all.
At least, that's what the cynics think.
Or, some may say, the intervention of the Lord?
If she, Maria Lori, that dark morning
back three hundred years ago,
had not called to her husband:
'Come see the weeping Christ ...'
(Real tears, she swore, had come to streak the statue's face)
and hubby, also credulous, came, marvelled,
saw them too
(Yes, hard to credit it, and why should we?)
this story wouldn't still be told today.

But friends and neighbours flocked in awe,
cures quite miraculous were seen,
and soon the wooden statue was removed
into the tiny timber chapel that they built at Wies,
and pilgrims from afar began to come.

Amazing how the desperate believe.
I see it every day.
Miracles and masses – a bit of healing on the side –
that never goes amiss. I've had a stroke or two of luck;
the ones who throw away their sticks and frames,
or suddenly can hear my voice.

Sisters and brothers, you in pain who suffer, come.
I make no claim to heal, but bring your sick to me.
Through me sometimes is channelled power
just as it was in days of old. Have faith, and pray.

Sometimes as in those early days at Wies it happens,
sometimes the sick are healed, or so it seems.
Today they come from far away, and so it was in Wies
three hundred years ago.

But what I really warm to is the next event –
the triumph of good sense and vision.
That abbot of the monastery at nearby Steingaden!

He seized his chance. You cannot tell me
that he didn't have an eye for possibilities of gain.
Why else invest in such an enterprise?
The scale of building this cathedral
out in the country just to house a statue!

His sense, his pragmatism, his feel for what
would be appropriate, in getting local craftsmen on the
  job –
I wonder when he realised, if ever, what he had begun?

For those two brothers Zimmerman, Dominikus and
  Johan,
both famous for their art and craftsmanship, now made
the Wies a life's work, drew others from their circle –
Albrecht, Sturm, Verhelst, Mages, and Bergmuller –
names now forgotten, but they live again in altars,
frescoes, stucco work that they created.

Oh yes, a canny man, that abbot. The church
has always needed men of vision, who understand
the masses' need, something to give hope,
someone to worship.

I look around me at the crowds who enter,
some to gaze while others sit, heads bowed,
in pews in silent prayer.

Who can discriminate, and say one man's devotion
will carry more weight than another's?
I read again the words of Peter Dörfler
on the screed we have been given:
he called the Wies
a 'bit of heaven in a suffering world.'

That nails it, I suspect.
For people need to feel that heaven is possible,
that for them too a better life can be assured.

My job, for that vast audience of viewers
(and it's vast! I check the ratings weekly!)
is to give them hope.

So if crowds come today to gaze upon that wooden statue
they have no expectations of Christ's tears,
although he stands here pitiful and scourged,
in chains and bruised. They come to marvel at
the wonders of the church that houses him.

And if they wish to give, to purchase relics,
whose right is it to say them nay?
For relics are a memory trigger,
one way of crystallising faith,
and many need this prop,
for simple souls cannot exist in abstract worlds;
they need the comfort of the tangible.
If others, like the Abbot, saw this
as investment, a way of guaranteeing some reward,
do we then have the right to criticise?

I have no argument with this.

When, in a rush of heart's devotion,
my followers, and there are many
in my family of faith,
decide to purchase books I've written,
or offer money to assist the work I do,
should I assume the right to say
this should not be?

I give them hope. I fill them with conviction
a good life can be theirs, both prosperous
and happy. If, so imbued, they go into the world,

confident, secure, I see a lot of merit in the principle
of self-fulfilling prophecy.

Then should I not accept my own reward?
The good book tells us that
'The labourer is worthy of his hire!'
I labour for them
and take their offerings without qualm.

Each of you, my dear dear friends, must recognise your role.
If God now puts it in your heart to help, to join us
in fulfilling our part in God's plan, make that commitment now.
Pick up your phone and call. Each small donation helps.
Our operators wait for you. God waits for you to call.

This is God's work I do, and he rewards me. So let them
hold enquiries, mount commissions, call me to account,
I know it is not me for whom the Scourged Christ wept.

Dear brothers and sisters, my dearly beloved
sisters and brothers, are you lonely, are you distressed?
Tonight I bring you a message of joy and love.
You need never feel alone again. Just hear my words,
allow yourselves to sink into the peace I bring.

Caroline

We passed him on the rising path
that leads up to this place.
'Checking out the opposition?'
John murmured in my ear,
for he stood there, that fake
(I saw him on TV one night,
one of those nights I waited,
waited, waited, recognising finally
it was in vain. Rob would not come.
I didn't find much comfort
in his words, though I admit
the honey tongue and reassuring voice
had some appeal. Seductive stuff.)

Now he stands looking at the stalls
of relics, souvenirs.

'Wonder if he'll buy a few for
show and tell on his next series?'
I said.

John laughed. We get on well.
I know he's interested in me.
Another man who has a history
of marriages behind him.
Another Rob. Women are fools
to fall for men like this.
I am a fool. But just for Rob.

We wait outside the church,
shake out umbrellas.
No summer weather this.

Can only hope tomorrow's play
performance will be better.

Look back, and see down near our bus
two figures standing.

'Who's with the driver?' John asks me.

'Strange guy. Ex-army maybe. Won't talk
about it, though.'

TOMMO: THE YEOMAN'S TALE

And he was clad in cote and hood of grene;
A sheef of pecok-arwes brighte and kene
Under his belt he bar ful thriftily,
(Wel coulde he dress his takel yemanly ...)

This yeoman wore a coat and hood of green,
And peacock-feathered arrows, bright and keen
And neatly sheathed, hung at his belt the while
— for he could dress his gear in yeoman style ...

Reasons why men go to war?

I'd like to say
I didn't have a choice.

In one way that was true.
When numbers came up in the ballot –
Christ! how those lottery balls rolled round –
breaths held suspended.
Mothers prayed.
If you were there, your date of birth,
no pretty invitations.
You got
those call-up papers
pretty damn quick smart.

Bit like the olden days.
I've read about it.
Back then the peasants did what they were told,
and if their lord went into battle,
it wasn't
'Would you like to come?'
No way.

184

You went and followed on,
no matter how you felt, behind his banner.

Just like that day at Pucka –
we'd finished rookie training.
The Sarge gave us a choice alright!
I still can hear his voice.
'All you fucking bastards
who don't want to go
to fucking Vietnam,
get over there!'

The only conchie who was willing to break ranks
got such a hard time from the rest of us –
and anyway, he ended up in gaol –
I look back now
and sometimes think
perhaps he was the only really brave man there.

Free choice!
Not when Sarge offered:
'Field force ... or Domestic?'
we knew which one to take.
By then we'd learned!
The hist'ry books all say
that we were volunteers.
Yeah.
Hist'ry often gets it wrong.

We'd gone in quite excited, I'll admit.
Hell, I was only twenty.
Keen to get away from Mum
and home.

So tripping down to Mangalore,
and then to Puckapunyal
big adventure.

Took twenty weeks of training ...
not quite so sure by then.
The marching, weapons drill,
care of weapons – yeah, I see the need for that.

But everything designed
to grind the spirit out of us.
They didn't want free thinkers.
The army wants the plodders,
those who'll follow orders.
Take morning runs those bastard corporals
sent us on.

'Up Tit Hill fast, you pack of losers ...'
Back again.
'Too slow. Now do it all again, and faster.
You'd be dead meat if this was Nam!'

Again.

'Now this time bring me back a stone.
Yeah. Get going, mother-fuckers!'

Back again. Panting.
Sweat pouring off.
Give him the stone.

He takes it. Sneers.

'Wrong stone.
Got wood between your ears,
you useless prick?
This time you get the right one!
Pick up your feet and go!'

Can't quite work out why
I'm thinking all this now.
A long way back. Gone –

but not forgotten, as they say.
If any Vietnam vet can say
he's put it all behind him,
tell him from me
that he's a bloody liar.
We can't forget.

Sure wasn't what we had expected.
But training was OK.
They sent me up to Townsville,
to join a service corps.
I'm good with trucks, so this was fun.
A cowboy life in Lavarack, truck convoys,
camping out at night.
Even jungle training in Canungra,
playing war.
It almost seemed like games.

Last night I had a real bad night.
Nothing new in that.
They're all bad nights, and worse
if I don't take my pills.
But last night I was back again,
and terrified.
Took long hours talking to the shrinks
before I'd tell them that.
How scared I'd been.

The jungle's like a beast;
It breathes its menace every move you make.
The rubber trees in all their rows – you never knew
just where the Cong were hiding. And even worse
the paddy fields. No cover there. You couldn't dare
put down your foot without the fear next minute
hidden mines would take you straight to hell.
Another hell, that is.

No wonder I still get night sweats.
But last night other things came back.

Especially the child ...

Forget last night.
I'll think about today.
I'd got to talking to the driver of our bus,
the one who brought us on this tour
this afternoon.

Now that I'm stuck with being here –
still can't believe I actually came –
I joined the group our tour guide organised.
Prefer to stick with people.
Can't stand the things I think about
alone.

'You'll find the Wies most interesting.'
That was what she said.
I didn't have a clue what it would be.
But when we got here and I saw it was
another church, I thought hell no;
I'll just wait till they all come back.

Driver standing near the bus;
we had a smoke together.
His English not too good,
and my few words of German,
but we managed.
'You from around these parts?'
Told me he's always lived
in Oberammergau –
he has to, to be in the play.

'You're in the play!' I was surprised.
And showed it.
'But you drive buses.'

He laughed. 'This I do also.'
Seems almost everyone who lives here
takes part on the performance days.
'Tomorrow in the Spielhaus, at the play.
There you look for me.'

'But you don't have long hair, long beard?'

I'd seen the others round the village.
The postman with his long hair flying in the wind
riding on his bike from house to house.
'He's Peter in the play,'
explained our guide.

But this man was clean-shaven, cropped quite short.

' Roman. Soldier in army in Jerusalem.'

That made sense. I knew they were an occupying force.
Bit like we'd been.
Not quite.
We'd only gone to help the South
fight for their freedom from the Commies.

'Three times I play this part.
Before, my father have it.'

That too made sense.
I'd heard that roles are sometimes
passed on in a family, fathers to their sons.

'So in the play, what do you do?'

He gestured.
There was no mistaking it.
He hammered nails into the hands and feet,
and helped to haul the cross upright.

I flinched. I couldn't help it.

And I have seen
some pretty horrible things on battlefields.

The times we were sent in next day
to strip the bodies of the dead VC.
Sometimes young boys.
Or men with photos of their wives,
their girlfriends, children.
Letters. Papers. Their ID.
We had to grit our teeth. We knew our job.
The Army wanted these.
Intelligence, they said.
So when the smoke of battle cleared,
we were the crows
who picked at their dead bodies.
That's how it felt.

I had to ask.
'How do you feel on stage?
What is it like to do these things?'

He shrugged and smoked on stolidly.
'It is what I am told to do.
It is my ... part. My duty.
Not to like. Someone must do.'

I've heard that one before.
It makes me spew.
He told me that, the night I went in,
drunk and shaking,
said to my CO I wanted out.
I said I'd had enough of orders,
told him about
the young girl in the doorway
in that village we were cleaning out.
It was a place, they said,
that hid the Cong –

the yellows, the fish breath,
we'd learned to hate,
the charlies, gooks, the slopes,
'the only good Cong are the dead'uns' – oh yeah,
they'd taught us well.

But when we looked at bodies,
sometimes young boys, they didn't seem
so different from the mates we had at home.

I stood there with the driver, looking at that church,
all white and gold, all pure and beautiful.
'You do not wish to see?' he asked.

Shook my head. 'Don't do the churchy stuff.'

'But you come here?'

Even if we'd had the language,
I doubt I would have tried to tell him why.

For that's another story, and it's not my own.

It's Jogger's tale, and it's for Jogger
that I've come.
Those last days in the hospital –
all very well for doctors to say emphysema …
we all now know that many things
that happen to us are from causes
that the army won't admit to.
Those tanks
with orange stripes along the side –
'Yeah,
got to clear the ground. If we can strip it bare
we won't have Cong troops hiding there.'
Sounded real plausible, but Agent Orange
took its toll
on more than just those villages and crops.

No wonder that my mates now worry for their kids.
Their children. That's the worst of it.
They say 'What goes round comes round.'
So now our kiddies suffer like their dads.

I don't believe that Jogger's problem's
quite so easy to account for.
'Ah, a smoker all his life!'
Too many of our chaps have lungs
that just don't work …
And not the smokers only.

We went back many years,
Jogger's been my mate since training in Canungra.
I was a Barnes; he was a Baynes.
We sort of landed
everywhere together.
And found we got on pretty well.

Got invalided out together too.
He never quite got over it.
No charges laid. It was a clear AD.
An accidental discharge … had a few of those.
We prided ourselves on the fact
that we weren't like the Yanks.
Those stupid buggers kept
their rifles at their sides.
Not us.
We knew to have them
always at the ready.
Swing them side to side.
Never be parted from your weapon.
They drilled that into us right from the start.
Funny,

it was almost the thing that I found hardest
after I demobbed.

The sense of emptiness and guilt.
I didn't have my weapon any more.
Something important missing from my life.

But there we were, a nasty day,
rain and steamy heat,
uneasy on patrol, and on the watch.
Slipped through undergrowth,
rifles swinging,
ready for a sign of movement,
Somehow
Jogger knocked his safety catch.
With that movement
fired.
And just bad luck, pure luck.

We all saw Kevin fall.

It was his first patrol, and down he went.
No question. 'Accidental discharge' –
it was clear.
but Jogger went to pieces.
So they sent him home.

I never knew how bad it was for him.
We never talked
about these things.
I knew he'd gone back to the church.
He always was a good RC.
Used to do the garden at St Pat's sometimes,
days when he was sober,
and even did some upkeep on the place.
But never,
drunk or sober,
talked of Nui Dat,
and what had happened
there.

Until that last week in the hospice.
Then he told me
how he'd made a promise to the priest
that he would do a penance.
He'd make a pilgrimage to this place,
Oberammergau, and ask forgiveness here.

I looked surprised, I guess.
Knew he was religious, knew that
they'd tried hard to get him off the plonk,
but this was taking it a bit too far.
Especially when I heard the rest.

'Won't make it, Tommo.
Doc says I'm a goner.'

He stopped to cough, and nurses hurried in to fix
the tubes. 'Can't get to Oberammergau.
But you go for me.
Tell them you've come in my place.'

'Tell who? Religion's not my thing,
you know that, mate.'

He took no notice. 'Get the box.
It's in the cupboard there.'

I got it out. Old battered tin chest.
Looked like an old tea tin.

'I've put aside the money. It's next year.
You go for me.'

Another coughing fit. Again the nurse came in.
She looked concerned.
'You'll need to go. He has to rest.'

But Jogger wasn't having that.
'See girlie, look at this.

I want to give my mate this box,
and everything that's in it.
You be a witness. It's for him.'

She looked a bit surprised.

But so was I, when I got home
and counted what he'd saved.
Must have taken him
a long long time. Important to him.
That was clear.
But hell! Me do this churchy thing!
I shook my head.
I'd have to tell him
someone else would need to go.

Couldn't do it in the end.
Next time I saw him
it was when they phoned me,
said to come. And quickly.
Wouldn't last too long.
He grabbed my hand
and clutched it like a drowning man.
Could hardly speak.
But gasped it out. 'You promise, mate.'
I waited –
coughing racked him –
but he battled on.
Always a battler, Jogger.
One of those who won't give up.
'Promise! Promise me you'll go.'
Gasping.
The white stuff coming from his mouth.
I couldn't turn him down.
I nodded.
'Say it!' he sort of gurgled.
So I did. He knew I'd keep my word.

He sort of shuddered, choked.
The nurse looked at me,
and I knew that he was gone.

Still not sure just what I'm meant to do here.
Say some sort of prayer, I guess.
But what I'm praying to
I wouldn't know. And what good
it will do. It's all the same.
They're dead.
Kevin, laughing with us in the mess, dead
at Jogger's hand, all those boys whose bodies
we pawed over, that young child in the doorway ...

She's the one I try to keep away.

That morning
when we cleared her village,
nest of Cong they'd told us.
Flush them out. It's them or us.

That flicker of a figure in the doorway,
so I fired.
Next thing the scream. Christ,
how that scream still rings each night in dreams!
The old woman, screaming, holds the body out
for us to see.
Seven, eight she might have been.
Long dark hair swinging in the air,
blood pouring
from the shattered chest.
And still the woman
screamed.
And screams.

Jogger and I – we never talked about it.
We never shared our nightmare nights.

But sometimes eyes reveal more than you mean
to show. Kevin, the child, all those bodies
we had seen – no way they'd let us go.
They came back with us on the plane.

They watched us as we stripped and put on civvy gear.

'Better not wear uniforms, you lads.
It gets a bad reception back at home.
Too many people now against the war.
Marches and all. Protesting.'

Puzzling. And unfair.
We hadn't wanted to be there.
We'd hated what we did.
We'd only followed orders.
But now they spat and jeered
if anyone was mad enough
to get out on the streets in uniform.
No honour
for returning vets.

Respect?
No way! They hated us.
And showed it. Even families.
Maybe they were glad
to have us back,
but still found us
embarrassing.

We paid the price all right for government mistakes.
Our lives were shot to pieces,
as surely as those others we'd destroyed.
I look into the mirror,
see that twitching eye,
the shaking in my hand.

They try to sweep it all away with pensions –
Yeah, we're disabled, sure enough.
No normal lives for us.
At least I wasn't married, Jogger neither.
We didn't have to go through what the others did.
Not many marriages survived what
we brought back with us.
And then when sickness
started, and we came to see
just how long term
our punishment would be …
no wonder that
we turned to anything to blot it out.
We never blamed
the ones who chose a swifter exit –
perhaps
theirs was the wisest way.

So what do you think now about it all, my driver friend?
For thirty years you've nailed that figure to the cross,
then hoisted him towards the sky.
Does he haunt your dreams too?
Or can you simply say, as soldiers
always have, for centuries long past,
and more to come:
'I followed orders …'
and forget it all?

Caroline

The rain has stopped. Clear evening.
The stars shine down – those lines
from Jacobean tragedy still
epitomise this life.

We're puny creatures in this universe.
But there above,
no matter what,
still the stars shine down.

Dinner over, my friends have all dispersed.
Some out, exploring little streets,
the shops that cater to these tourists
eager for their souvenirs, mementos
of a time they may wish to recall.

Is that all that we take away from this?

What will I take from here?

A crowd of characters to people
my imagination? A swag of stories,
some bestowed upon me, others
left as embryos to grow
inside my mind?

A night for walking, thinking,
wondering.

JOSEF: THE PLOWMAN'S TALE

A trewe swinker and a good was he,
Livinge in pees and parfit charitee.
God loved he best with al his hole herte
At alle tymes, thogh him gamed or smerte ...

He was an honest worker, good and true,
Living in peace and perfect charity,
And, as the gospel bade him, so did he,
Loving God best with all his heart and mind

The shop itself was small, just like the others.
We'd set off walking, down the Passionswiese,
round into Dorfstrasse, all these little streets,
the houses with their painted walls,
the scenes from fairy tales,
and many Bible stories.

And shops!

I'd never have believed how many little shops
there are along these roads –
all full of souvenirs. And eager crowds!
The ones I liked were wood carvers – so many here.
But Mick and Bill said 'Tourist rubbish!'
Set off for the pub, quick smart.

We'd come out after tea time, just the three of us,
to have a quick look-see at what the shopping offered.
They wanted presents to take home to wives
and grand-children.

I'd guess I'd be the same,
If Phyl was still alive,

but doesn't seem much point these days.
She used to always buy the gifts
for Christmases and birthdays.
To tell the truth I wouldn't even know
what I should get the kids.

In any case, the blokes all said quite firmly
this stuff was wooden
so customs wouldn't let us bring it in;
for sure they'd confiscate it all
to keep Australia free from foreign bugs.
I think I read that too.

Off they went to get a beer or two;
I'd have to say that German beer is real good stuff.
But me, I wanted to stay on and look some more.

Always been int'rested in wood.
My old dad taught me how to carve,
left me his tools.
More than I'll have to leave to anyone.

It was a sort of hobby. Made some real good pieces.
Rocking horses for the kiddies,
back when they were little tackers.
They loved those horses.
Now their kids have them.
At least that's something they'll inherit.
But not much more.

I like these shops. The workrooms at the back,
the smell of sawdust, wood chips,
old men who sit and carve.
They scarcely looked at me except to nod a greeting.
Walls stacked with crosses, signs and Bible texts,
Auf Gott vertrauen wir …
In God we trust!

Not any more I don't.
He's let me down.

The shelves on shelves of animals!
You name it, and it's there. Sheep,
pigs and cows, and camels, tortoises,
the cats and dogs of farmyards, all so real.

You'd see at once the care and time and love
went into carving all this stuff.
The tables, crammed with Christmas goods,
those whirlygigs that show the manger scene,
the shepherds, the wise men –
the ones that spin around when you light candles
under windmill sails.

I spent a lot of time with those,
rememb'ring Christmases when I was young,
and Christmas Eves at church, hot summer nights,
and carols in the little wooden country church.

But specially I liked the animals this bloke had carved.

I held some lambs and calves; they were so good
you knew the carver had put heart into his work.
If Phyl had been alive, I'd risk the Customs people
and take some back to her.

'See love,' I'd try to tell her,
I had to shoot the sheep,
you know I had to do it.
I brought you these instead.'

Fair broke her heart – and mine –
that morning I went out and shot the lot.

No choice. They were half dead of thirst in any case.
And scrawny. No fodder,

and no chance of buying more.
The bank had made that clear.

I saw them look at me,
each animal, each time I raised the gun.
I think it was the way I'd looked
at Wally Mitchell, that last morning in the bank.
We both knew it was hopeless.

He had that look all bankers get
when they're about to pull the plug.

'Look Joe,' he hated saying it, I knew.
'It can't go on.
You haven't had a decent crop in years.
Your animals are dying on their feet.
We don't know when this drought will break.
If ever. I can't help you any more.
I've had my orders from the city heads.'

I know what's coming next.
He doesn't have to tell me.

Foreclosure's not just looming in the distance.
It's right here.
As soon as I get back, it's time
to bite the bullet, walk away from years
of family history, see the bank take everything
that near two hundred years of Schmidtkes have built up.

There'll be a clearing sale, I guess.
I'll see our bits and pieces, our tractors,
headers, harvesters, even the old wagons
that our forebears used to do the trek
from where they landed in the south
across the miles in search of farming land to settle –
all that history will go. I don't know
what my granddad would have said.

'You're fond of animals?
They're beautifully made, aren't they?'
She caught me by surprise. I hadn't heard her
come into the shop, but there she was.
I'd seen her round, of course.

She seemed a friendly woman,
talked to everyone. I hadn't realised
that I was standing thinking,
holding those two lambs, remembering.
I felt a fool.

But she smiled understandingly,
picked up a little dog. 'My dad,' she said,
'He used to have a dog like this.
He called it Blue –
a sheepdog on his father's farm.'

I nodded. 'They're good dogs.'

She smiled. 'I always went there for the holidays
from school. I loved that place.'

'Where was it?'

'Riverina area. Where do you come from?'

'I'm in the Wimmera, m'self.
Family's been there for years.'

The old man in the back began to move.
Took in the board from out the front.
Started to close the shutters.

'I think it's closing time,' she said.
'Look, my name's Caroline.
I'm with the tour group too.
I'm going to get coffee first and then go back.

Like to join me for a cup of something?'

I thought that it would be unfriendly to say no,
so next thing we were sitting in a cafe –
they have them everywhere you look.

'I'd really rather have a cup of tea,'
I said. 'Too late for coffee for me.'

The waitress came up, dressed the part,
her blond plaits swinging, and her apron
checked with red and white.
Reminded me of Lena as a little girl.

'Kaffee, bitte, und eine Tasse Tee,'
I ordered.

The woman with me looked impressed.
'Your German's good.'

'It should be. I was brought up speaking it.
My background's German. The old folks
all spoke deutsch at home.'

I was a bit surprised to see that Caroline
was nodding in agreement: 'Mine too,'
she said. 'But that was grandparents.
My mum and dad spoke only English with us.
I wish they hadn't –
I'd like to speak it like you do.'

I guess I felt we had a bit in common.
Somehow I found her easy to be with, to talk to.
Like a daughter. I could have been
with Lena having coffee.

She seemed to want to know about me and my life.
How had I come to be here, on this trip. And so on.

Somehow with her they didn't seem
such nosy questions. Looking back,
I'm quite surprised how much I told her as we sat.

About the way the kids had all clubbed in
to buy this trip for me.
It was a birthday present.

She raised an eyebrow. 'Special birthday?'

'Sixty.' I'm not ashamed to tell my age.
I reckon that's a woman thing.

'Nice gift!' she commented. 'Just over here?
Or travelling long? Why this place?
Are you religious?'

Funny question that. Am I religious?
Phyl was, for sure.
We never missed a Sunday at the church,
that was engrained in both of us.
That's how we brought the kids up too.

Not that they stick to it these days.
I've never thought about it much.
Just went along, and always did my bit.
Put in the offering every Sunday,
helped with communion when it was my turn,
made sure we always had devotion
in the evening after dinner.
Did my bit for God.

But now I'm wondering:
what's he done for me?
Did he make crops grow, send the rain we needed,
keep the banks from off my back?
I'm not sure God is on my side.
Why should I be on his?

Bit strange, this trip to Oberammergau.
It was an extra that the family added on,
because they thought it would be something
that I'd really like.
Can't see the point, myself.
But it's the last part of my time away.
God's let me down. That's the way
I feel. But that's my business — none of hers.

And so I told her how it started —
how the main trip was to Poland,
something that I'd always wanted,
to see the places where my ancestors had been.

'Poland? I thought that you were German background.'

'Yeah, but that bit of Germany is Poland now.
Things change.
It used to be Silesia. Not any more.'

Things changing ... that's too true.
Our home. I wonder who'll be on our land
this time next year.
Or will they let the old place just fall down?
It's possible.

'So did you find the place? In Poland?'

I brought myself back to the present,
told her how I'd had a photo of the house
my grandfather, a hundred years ago, had left,
and armed with that and just a German village name,
I'd found my way through Poland to the area.

'That must have been a long shot —
looking for one house from just a photograph?'

'Didn't think I had a snowflake's hope in hell,
but listen to what happened ...'

The friendly *Gasthaus* owner in that Polish town,
who spoke good German, my first bit of luck,
and the way – I shook my head in wonder!
I still can't quite believe it – the way
he knew the village, knew the very house, and told me
that his sister owned it now.

I glanced at Caroline, saw the look of disbelief.
'Y'know, can't quite credit it myself.
It's just amazing that it happened.
But it did.'

'You went there?'

'I sure did. They were real welcoming.
The brother – German-speaking one – translated
for us, and the Polish couple gave us cake and coffee.
It felt good. Good to be in touch with roots.'

Roots. We all need something that will give
a feel for who we are and where we come from.
We need to know our past.

How can I let our past be taken from us?
Pass to others' hands?
It was a trust to me, and now I've let it go.

And not as if it wasn't wanted!

He, the boy, young Max, he wanted it.

Not like his dad. The farm meant
nothing much to Colin.
Strange to have a son who didn't care.
He was keen to get away.

But then his son, he knew.
Max knew the call of land.
He had it in his blood.
From when he was a little chap,
always out with me. No matter what the weather,
what the job, he wanted to be part of it.
I'd tell him 'One day, laddy, this is yours.'
That was what he wanted.
That's what he's preparing for.

How can I tell him, next time he comes back,
that all these years at college learning agriculture,
all the improvements, plans he has,
all this can come to nothing.

Because I've lost the farm for him.

No one knows. Not yet.
I haven't told the kids the truth –
of just how bad things are.
Or what the future holds.
Or doesn't hold.

I hadn't meant to tell this woman any of it.
Yet somehow, found I wanted to. Not much,
just that I'd soon be selling up, and moving on.

Too many bad years. Not just me, but lots of others.
All giving up and giving in. All failures.

Oh yeah, the government is very thoughtful!
They bring in their psychologists to help us through.
What do they think? A few quick conversations
make it all much better? They know where they can put
their talk and their psychologists. Young city slickers,
Think a degree gives them an understanding how we feel?

And nor would she – this Caroline.

But even so I found that I could tell her
of the night I sat, rifle on the table,
and tried to think it through.
Phyl gone, crop failed.
Again.
The early promise of at last a better year
now flattened in the storms that hit our parts.

That put the final kibosh on it all. So what was left?
Sweet bugger all. Why not just finish it and go?

But then, the kids. What would they think?
Somehow I found that it still counted.

Maybe I'd lost the farm, maybe young Max
would never get his chance, his dream,
but their reaction? What would they think of me?
That's not the stuff we're made of.

All those years ago the old folks took their wagons
and their bullock trains and set off
searching for new land.

They stuck it out. They didn't say 'too hard'!

I may have given up on God, but giving up on life
is something else. I'll wait and see.

'So Caroline, tomorrow's the Big Day –
the Passion Play.

I dunno why I'm here – except I have a ticket.
That's not much of an answer for you. But it's all
that I can give you. I'm here because I'm here.

Yes, I bought the little sheep. It's for my grandson.
I'll get it home somehow.
The lad likes sheep. It's nothing much.
But it's the only thing that I can give him now.

Best we get back and get some shut-eye.
Tomorrow's going to be a long long day.'

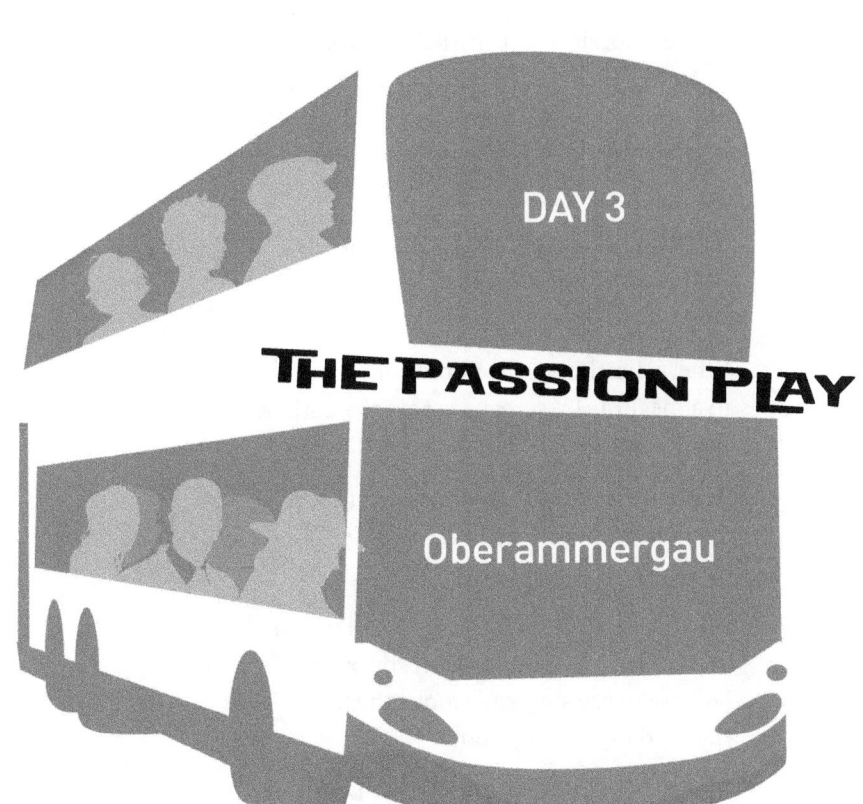

DAY 3

THE PASSION PLAY

Oberammergau

Caroline – breakfast

'You'd never spot her for a winner.'
That's what John said to me
the first night at the Munich gathering.

I have a horrible feeling that she overheard.
But when I looked again, she turned away
and seemed to be absorbed in looking
at the paintings on the wall.

She seems to be a loner.
People, by and large, trying hard to be
convivial. She stood alone,
ill-at-ease.

Where did she get the gumption
to appear on TV screens across the nation,
night on night?

Amazing that the crowds so took to her.
Perhaps her very ordinariness?

Maybe in all those living rooms
they could identify with this small woman,
mousy-haired, with glasses, shy but eager.
I'd have to say she really looks the part,
the stereotype librarian.

And yet she won that cooking competition,
and crowds were happy for her!
Another triumph of the underdog?

Our national obsession that tall poppies
ought to be cut down? She's certainly
not tall, and definitely not
a poppy either.

I took the chance that night
to talk to her, and asked her how
she'd known about this tour. It seems
to be a good way to discover
why people are involved, and sometimes
even what they hope to find.

But there was little to be gained from her.
A reference, very vague, to her grandmother,
and just how often she had talked about this place.

The woman's death was fairly recent –
that much I gathered – so perhaps this may
have been the spur to coming here.

We talked a little of the contest, and
her future plans. Again, it was all vague.
A European tour of restaurants and cooking classes;
she's been to Italy to study truffles.
'Not France and Périgord?' I queried.
But here she was quite definite. 'No, Alba and
white truffles.' She seems to know her stuff.

But one who won't be easy to find out about.
I watch her now at breakfast, and wonder . . .

The others straggle in.

Anticipation in the air. Today's the day
that we've been waiting for, but still
the morning hours to fill.

I'll check my mail, but with no lift of heart.
Anticipation slowly dies. No word from Rob.

LINDA: THE COOK'S TALE

A cook they hadde with hem for the nones ...
He coude roste, and seethe, and broille, and frye,
Maken mortreux, and wel bak a pye.

They had a Cook with them who stood alone ...
And he could roast and seethe and broil and fry,
Make good thick soup and bake a tasty pie.

So. This is German *Frühstück*.

I find myself appraising it –
professionally – what a German breakfast
offers. The standard breads and cheeses,
good variety of wursts, pedestrian boiled eggs
each swaddled in its small checked jacket.
But then, more interesting, bowls of meats
and fish, the *Fleischsalat*s and *Fischsalat*s
that I've been waiting for. They're good.

Interesting, the way the others cast
those covert glances at me, every time
we find ourselves at yet another table.
As if they think that I must be expert
when it comes to food. I try to look
judicious, and carefully evaluate each plate
that's put before me.

Not hard to do in Germany,
where restaurants on this tour
are clearly chosen for *Gemütlichkeit*,
that comfortable home-type atmosphere,
and not cuisine ...

I overheard them talking
at the first reception.

'You'd never spot it,'
said a man – good looking, tall and dark,
intimidating with his air of arrogant ease –
to his companion, equally superior,
'but she's the chef who won first place
on last year's cooking show. You know the one;
it seemed that everyone was watching it
each night. And news in every daily paper!
I guess she's spending all the cash she won.'

He's right, of course. These weeks in Europe
I see as my reward for all that anguish.

Let no one tell you that emotions on those shows,
whatever form they take, are fake. I know
our competition took more out of all of us
than nightly audiences ever saw.

In fact, much more than ever was selected
for entertainment of the crowds
who followed the intensities
of highs and lows we suffered.
Tears, laughter, the elation, the despair
they were allowed to see was nothing
when I think back to moments
that were never shown on nightly screens.

The nights when friends were in elimination heats
we agonised for them.
The night I faced elimination was, I think,
the worst night of my life.

I'm quite sure it's the same –
I've come to understand it – for all those other shows.
Dancers, singers, biggest losers, opera stars,

renovators who take on old wrecks –
these shows, so called 'reality TV',
just skim the surface of the true realities
behind the culled synthetic moments
that our audiences love.

I found it hard.
By nature, I'm a private person,
not one to wear my heart on sleeve
for all to gape at.
It was one more thing that she taught me,
'Keep your feelings to yourself!
Don't show the whole world when you're hurt.
Look invulnerable. That's the aim!'

She was my grandmother,
chief figure in my life so many years..

Still now I find I use her words,
those age-old slogans that she lived by,
teaching me to do the same.

'Wear out; don't rust out!' That came often.
'If a job's worth doing, it's worth doing well.'
Her principles. She lived by them,
and now I find I do the same.

Oma – she chose that name, you know.
The product of her German heritage.
'I won't be Grandma,'
she asserted at the first-born grandson's christening.
'And as for Nanny! No thank you!
It makes me sound a goat.' So Oma she became.

For Oma was the one who raised me,
instilled in me the principles she lived by,
comforted and cared for me in all those years
of my abandonment.

It's due to her that I am here today.
She was the one who taught me how to cook.
And what is more,
to love the food I make.
For that's the secret she imparted to me.
Food cooked with love,
the wish to care for others,
that's what counts.

They asked me often, all those weeks after my win,
in interviews for women's magazines,
in radio talk-back, in follow-up appearances,
guest chef on cooking shows,
just what I thought my secret of success.

What school, they kept demanding, did I follow?
Was I *nouvelle cuisine*, or had I moved like many
to *cuisine minceur*?

Tempting to join their game, to talk of complex sauces,
from mousselines to bechamels, best way to make a roux,
the rich madeira sauce of Normandy to Italy's Sauce
    Genovese
for fish, of sorrels, dusting, soils,
the virtues of black truffles from the Perigord
compared with San Giovanni's whites …

But I preferred to stick with honesty,
and talk about the real respect for the ingredients
that I'd been taught all those years back
in Oma's kitchen.

I see myself,
a small sad child, but happy in the warmth
of the old Aga stove, where breads rose slowly
and the lightest sponges floated from the oven.

I feel again companionship and love
as we beat eggs, creamed sugar with the butter –
always by spoon, of course – she didn't hold
with those short cuts that electricity might give.
Flour and spices sifted, till the kitchen filled
with aromatic and nostalgia-rousing smells.

For in those hours I could forget the gaping hole,
the wrenching sadness of my mother's loss,
the yearning for her bedtime kiss.
No wonder that for me, the kitchen was a haven,
and easy to see now, in retrospect,
how food's creation soon became a way
of bringing peace, a chance
to give to others happiness I did not have.

But these were memories I kept preserved and safe.
Not for the world to share.

Nor was the truth that I discovered only
when she felt that I was ready,
that mum whom I had mourned so long
was still alive, in fact had left us of her own free will,
and gone to someone else,
who wouldn't take her saddled with a child.

No wonder Oma kept it from me,
too hard a burden for that child to bear.
better I mourned a death than such desertion.

I sometimes wonder, if she'd stayed,
how different now my life might be.

At least I had the love of family,
those Sunday nights when everyone came home,
and we'd cook up a feast for uncles, aunts and cousins.

A source of joy, I learned that early,
for food could be a way of showing love.

Perhaps of buying it? That was a thought
whose cynicism I was yet to learn.
Perhaps it was the breeding ground in which
my dearest wishes found their start.
To cook for others.
That became the dream that I held on to.

It's natural that others on this tour
should be surprised to find out who I was.
I'm not exactly fame and fortune type,
and I've seen judges and selectors
raise a glance of real uncertainty
on whether I was suited for the show.

'A timid little thing,' I heard one say.
'I can't imagine she would ever get support.
No audience appeal.'

Perhaps it was my very ordinariness
that many people took to?
I knew just what I was,
resisted all attempts by make-up artists
to transform it.

Linda, a dull librarian who loved to cook.
No trappings and no big flamboyant gestures.
Just love of food and of the friends
I could give pleasure through it.

But, bit by bit, those people out there seemed
to warm to me.
To everyone's surprise, producers
most of all, I had acquired a following.

Made friends with others in the show,
and in that awful week when I was sent away,
loser to a bright young man
whose twitter fan club was impressive,
I found the public outcry of regret
a soothing of my soul.

And when, just two weeks later,
the lucky draw gave me a second chance,
the welcome back from others in the house
was more than compensation for the misery.

A good time to be home, those weeks,
with Oma who seemed older, frailer.
Something of the spring had left her steps.
She sat more in her favourite chair,
content to watch me cook, to reminisce.

She was so proud when I had passed the first audition.
And, truth to tell, she had good reason.
I never would have entered such a contest
without her urging and encouragement.

'You know you love to cook.
Look at the way you spend your time.
You hardly ever look at books that are not recipes;
you spend your time on internet research
or trying new concoctions.
What's more, they're always good.'

It's true. It was the focus of my life.

What else does a librarian of forty two
do with days that lack the closeness of a lover,
children, fulfilment of my youthful dreams?

I owed her for her love,
the years that she had tuned her life to me

and to my needs. I did not know, back then,
how little time she had, or how important
it would be to her to see me win this contest.

She'd always seemed so indestructible.
But now there was an odd uncertainty about her.
We were together constantly those weeks.
My leave from work was not yet up
and, disappointed as I was,
I wanted time to lick my wounds.

We talked.

I found that for the first time she was willing
to tell me more about my mum, that mystery figure
who had always lurked behind our lives.

There was a wistfulness in what she said.
And in her eyes.
'I'd like to see her, Lin, you know.
She is my daughter, after all.
No matter what.'

I felt a rush of anger.
Surely I had been more than a daughter to her.
Why should she want to resurrect the past?

'She's never made an effort to see us!'
I guess my voice was bitter. There was
a shadow of regret, I recognise it now,
that crossed her face before she answered.

'I'd made it clear, that if she did this thing,
went off and left you with me, that was it.
She was no child of mine.'

'It was the best thing that she could have done.
You've been a better mother to me than she ever was.'

My memories were dim, but I could still recall
the men, the drinking and the noise, the nights
of lying scared with blankets tightly pulled
above my head.

Abandonment had brought
a strange ambivalence. A yearning for the mum
I'd never really had, and deep relief to find myself
within a world of order, love, predictability.
The world my grandmother had given me.

Why would she now wish to revive the past?

'She's written to me, just last week. I haven't
answered yet. It's your decision, Lin. I won't
allow her to intrude into our lives unless
you say you're happy with it.'

I wonder now just why I was so adamant;
there was no yielding in my words.

More though, if I were honest,
jealousy also. I'd been the centre of her life
through all these years. Was I to watch another
walk into my place?

I slowly shook my head.
'I can't pretend that I'd be happy. Please
don't let her come.' I didn't look at her.
I didn't want to see the disappointment
in those faded eyes, the resolute set of the lips
that faced the implications of my words.

Besides, we had our plans. 'What will you do,'
she asked me once, 'if you should win?
How would you spend the money?'

I'd hardly dared to think ahead,
some deep fear, primitive,
a finger-crossing warding off of failure,
but now in answer to her question I admitted
the stray thoughts that I had allowed.

'I'd change my life. Resign. Travel first.
Do courses in the famous cooking schools of Europe,
and then, I hope, find work in kitchens here.
One day, perhaps, my own.'

Her eyes were full of distant dreams.
'You know, I've always wanted to do that,
to travel. One place that fascinated me
was Germany, to go there,
to see the Passion Play at Oberammergau.
Let's say you win, you should give thanks.
You could go there.'

It still hurts now to know that, two weeks later,
when unexpected second chances returned me
to the show, I was absorbed again in Sydney
and the house, in all those gleaming kitchens,
oddly smaller on the set than they appear
on countless television screens.

I revelled in the largesse of stocked pantry shelves,
in challenges that spurred such moments of invention,
in tremulous anxiety when judges,
faces considered and inscrutable,
raised first forkfuls,
in jubilant relief when smiles of approbation
meant I'd survived another round.

I called each night to tell her of the day,
give her a foretaste of the scenes she'd see
when each day's shooting went to air.

I scarcely noticed how her voice
had quietened, or heard the forcing
of the animation that she'd always shown.

I never heard the other voice
there in the background of the room.

'No, I won't come to Sydney for the Final.
I'd rather wait until you tell me later.
Too much stress for both of us.
You know I'm there with you in spirit.
As always.'

And then our ritual farewell, from childhood on,
as every night she tucked me into bed,
'Sleep well, and God bless you.'
How apt those last words were.

They were indeed her last words to me.
When, flushed and tearful with success,
I'd made the final speeches,
honoured her for all that she had taught me,
my first act was to call,
to lay my triumph at her feet.

Alarm grew when there was no answer.
I heard the phone ring out,
the answering machine kick in.
Her mobile? Off, of course.
She'd always hated it, accepted it
reluctantly at my insistence,
rarely switched it on.

I phoned a neighbour,
the panic in my voice quite clear,
as was her obvious reluctance
to give me the news.

'They took her in an ambulance.
She wouldn't go until tonight,
no matter what her daughter and the doctor said.
She wanted to be home
for when you called each night.
But she collapsed today,
and had no say in it.'

I was too late, of course.
While I had cooked that last and ultimate challenge,
she'd met her own.

No matter how I railed, they were all clear.
'She would not have you told.'

But that I can't forgive.
No chance to say goodbye.
To tell her what her love and care had meant to me.
To be with her,
and hold her hand as she had held mine all these years.

And even worse, to know that
she, my mother,
had been there instead.

She wants a reconciliation.
That's mockery beyond belief.

'I made my peace with Mum.
She wanted me to reestablish bonds with you ...'

Surely she's not so stupid as to think
I'd fall for that. I can't forgive her.
Not even so much her desertion of me,
all those years ago,
but far more this betrayal,
that she could be persuaded not to let me know.

Or maybe that was her idea. Perhaps Oma had
called for me, had wanted me there at the end,
and been denied. Who knows?

I can't forgive that woman –
I will not call her mother –
that she was with her at the end, not I.

But this at least I'll do.
This trip we'd talked about.
I'm doing what she wanted,
and honouring all that she was
in my own way.

Caroline

No email there, of course.
Well, none that counted.

I'd hurried to the Alte Post hotel,
put down my seven euros for the half hour
at their internet café (no one had warned me
of the lack of easy access
to an internet connection.)
Scrolled quickly down the inbox
and felt that old familiar lurch
of disappointment.
No sudden joy as his name
leapt out to my search.

At least, I thought, fighting back
the threat of tears, at least
a brief professional communication.
But then, would that have satisfied
my eager seeking eyes?

Is this the way I want my life to be?
The sparse and random highs,
the gulfs of disappointment, loneliness?

Ahead, the morning's grey skies
mirroring my mood.
I wander round the streets alone,
shrouded in misery.

JACK: THE SUMMONER'S TALE

A somnour was ther with us in that place ...
In daunger hadde he at his owene gyse
The yonge girles of the diocyse
And knew hir counseil, and was al hir reed.

There was a Summoner with us in the place ...
... by mere threat, this fellow could possess
the boys and girls of all the Diocese,
He knew their secrets and they went in dread.

Trinkets, baubles, ornaments.
Coloured lights and glittering stars.
Christmas music pounding through the air.

Every second shop, I'd swear,
another Christmas store.
Crowds flocking in,
jingling coins and flashing credit cards.

Bit different from those stories
of a manger in a stable.
Though plenty of those here
in wooden replicas
circling round
in countless scenes of the nativity.

'The morning is free time,'
– the tour guide's words.
'If I may make suggestion,
most visitors enjoy to buy,
especially the Christmas shops.'

The sort of places I should keep
well clear of, that I know.
Even here, in Oberammergau.

Too many children there.
Why court temptation?
Misery.

I know myself.

They warned me when they sent me packing –
Oh, discreetly done! 'We think it best,'
a smooth dismissal, 'that you resign
at once. Health reasons, we can say.'

They're good at that, these schools.
No whiff of scandal. And parents
never want their little darlings
tainted by the stories that might get around.

Not in my backyard.
It's classic NIMBY stuff.

They moved me quietly from school
to school, preferring not to look
too closely at the reasons why
I rarely stayed too long in any place.

I've always had the knack
of getting on with kids. They recognise
a teacher who is interested,
who takes them seriously, wants to know
just how they feel. They open up
like flowers in the sun
when someone shows them such attention.

Used to be a different world.
Then one could put an arm around
a crying child, and give some comfort.

Counsel troubled kids in rooms alone
in private, when the school day's done.

Not any more. These days
the moral watchdogs are on guard.
Suspicious breed.
A hint of human feeling
and you're out.

Kids would relax with me.
Tell me all their problems.
The things they couldn't talk
to mum or dad about.
Heart-breaking really, just how starved
of real affection many of them were.

You'd have to have a heart of stone …

They trusted me.
They'd drop in at my room
when things were bleak, or if they felt
alone and needy.

I could relate to that. Sometimes
there's comfort in a touch,
a bit of warmth, affection.
I gave them what they needed.
What I needed too.

No scandals.
No one wanted scandals.
A quiet move from school to school,
before complaints were aired.

I had my uses. Coached the swimming team,
ran chess, debating, did the magazine.
Activities I loved, and with my guidance,
so did they. So many misfits found with me
acceptance. And for some, affection.

Easy to lean close at desks with nubile girls.
Good to watch those trim young bodies
in the pool. And in the change room after.

Enough of this. It's on to business.
Presents for my sister's children.
They're fond of Uncle Jack. Back then
when they were small, I was the one
for horsey rides, or bedtime stories.

Until she said they were too big for that.
Looked at me, worried,
when she thought I couldn't see.
For old times sake I'll find a present
in these Christmas shops. And maybe
earn a hug when I get back.

But back to what?

A question. Somehow I think
there may not be another school.
This time they urged long service leave
on me. Suggested strongly I should

travel. For my health.

There was a boy, a troubled lad,
I'd tried to help. His problems
were too great. In spite of all my efforts
he could no longer cope.

A terrible moment for his father,
finding him like that. The memory
must haunt his nights. For all the questions
from police, no reason could be found.
He'd been to see me in the afternoon,
but I could throw no light on it.

Worried about his work?
A little. But no more than usual.

Other problems?
None that I was going to talk about
to crass outsiders.

'It must have caused you great distress,'
the head was non-committal.
'We know that you were close to him.'

And so long service leave and travel
were the outcome.

Fetched up here. A trip
that someone recommended.
Who?
Perhaps that last shrink chosen
by the school?

On with the present buying. Too much
to choose from.

Life is always full of choices.

I'm never sure that mine are right.

Caroline

I take it back. He called.
I should have realised
he wouldn't email.

We joked about it once.
Except I knew it was no joke.

Nothing in writing.
No evidence for jealous wives to find.

But this makes everything alright.

He's missing me. He finds a gap
that only I can fill. His life
is barren and he waits for my return.

So this was not a farewell gift.
He's waiting for me to come back.
Back to him.

NATHAN: THE SHIPMAN'S TALE

And, certainly, he was a good felawe ...
Of nyce conscience took he no keep.
If that he faught, and hadde the hyer hond,
By water he sente hem hoom to every lond.

And certainly he was an excellent fellow ...
Few were the rules his tender conscience kept.
If, when he fought, the enemy vessel sank,
He sent his prisoners home; they walked the plank.

A disappointing group, I'd have to say.
I'd looked them over, that first night in Munich.
Not at all what I'd expected.
I'd thought – well, given what it was –
that this would be a troop of lonely ladies,
just waiting for a man like me.

Hope springs eternal.

It's being here. It's walking down
these half-remembered streets,
that makes me feel alone.

Breakfast this morning. Got in late.
Forgot how Germans like to have life
run like clockwork.

One vacant seat.
Not one I would have chosen.
Next to that travel writer ...
She'd bailed me up the first night
back in Munich and I didn't fancy more.

A snooty little lady, up herself.
Too many questions.

'My first time in these parts?'

Told her that I'd been based in Munich
many years ago.

And then escaped;
went to get myself a drink.

Now trapped at breakfast; no way out.
She followed through alright.
'A pilot? With Lufthansa?'
'Lived here a year? Late seventies?
And had I been to Oberammergau before?'

Easiest to shake my head.
No way I'd tell her anything.
And nothing of that girl who still
sometimes I think about.

Not often.
I've blotted Liesel out quite easily.
So many others since those days.

None, I suspect, in this mob here.

Too many men, and not much talent
in the females. One there
I thought might have been possible.
Type I like. Wealthy widow,
but with her hooks into another bloke.

Not like the old days.
We could always pull them in.
Could always count on glamour.
Something about a pilot
seemed to have appeal.

Even later years, it worked.
Casually drop the words.
My work? A modest
'Yes, I used to fly. Jet pilot ...'
Amazing how it worked.

'Still flying? Your own plane?'

Got to retirement years
but kept the image polished.
Self-deprecating.
'Just a little single-engine job.
I only fly for fun, these days.'

It seemed to get them in,
Their eyes would widen. See past
the wrinkles and the greying hair,
latch on to what I used to be.
It was the hook I always used.
Saw me through my fifties, sixties.
Hard to give it up.
But when you're pushing seventy,
time to live on memories.
and maybe take whatever you can get.

'You lucky bugger!' That was Cliff
to me one night about ten years ago.
'You've never looked your age.'
Half enviously:
'You've never had a problem pulling birds.'

Think about him more and more these days.
Not just the times we shared
when we were young. Though these
are best to think about. Younger days –
before the rot set in.

Oberammergau.
Last time I came here, different world.
With Liesel then.

Woke up this morning at first light.
Night just the same as always.
Need to piss that gets you up and down
and makes the thought of solid sleep
a distant memory.

Other thoughts come crowding in at night.
Aches and pains, the grim reminders
that the body's giving up.
Not that I'm giving in to that.
I won't be put aside, not out to pasture
yet. Not for a long time yet.

No wonder that Cliff took it hard.
There's things that make a man feel
that he's passed his use-by date.

Looked around last night at dinner.
Dispiriting.
No comfort when you realise
you'd have to be the oldest in the room.

At least I've kept my hair.
So if the colour owes a bit
to Giovanni's art, there's no disgrace
in that. If women can, why not men too?

The dating game is harder though, these days.
I've tried them all. The agencies
with all their fancy names, the internet –
too easy there to find yourself
across the table from some dog –
Don't tell me photos never lie!

And then they look so desperate,
trying hard to be appealing.
I've had a few near-misses there.
(Though most of them well past
the misses' age they'd claimed to be.)

Try cruises, that was Jock's advice.
He'd found a swinging widow there
and settled down with her.
Not my style.
I've steered well clear of all that
holy wedlock stuff. Too many opportunities,
too many women asking for it,
in all those years and all those places.
A man'd be a fool to stick to one.

Came close a time or two. But no regrets.
Except perhaps for one. The only time
I thought I might get hitched.
Still think of her, and wonder.

Not surprising. Because I'm here
I think about her. Maybe I need
to put that round the other way.
Perhaps because I think about her
I've come here?

Saw it in the travel brochure when I booked
the trip. Brought back some memories.
Thought, oh to hell with it, I'll go back there,
I'll have another look.
The good old 'might have been.'
My German *Fräulein*.
See what thirty years have done
and what the place is like these days.

I'd met her on the Munich run –
Lufthansa, I was flying for back then.
A blonde haired, blue-eyed *Mädchen*,
Liesel, a real looker. Came from somewhere
round these parts. She was special.
Strange girl. I couldn't get her into bed.
Perhaps that was her charm. Not too available!

Couldn't make her out. These were the seventies.
Most birds were very willing. Not Liesel.
Something untouched about her. Made me feel
Protective. Believed her when she said
She'd never screwed around. Never.
I liked the thought of that –
I'd be her first.

Not many girls like that around.
I found it hard to understand.
So she explained about this play,
Her family in this place, this Oberammergau.
This thing they put on each tenth year.
The next year it would be the play.
She wanted to play Mary, like her mum
before her. And she had to be a virgin.

I laughed, but she was serious.
'Auditions?' She blushed.

'Yes. I must swear an oath,
that I have not been with a man.'

Plenty other girls about, and very willing.
Somehow they'd lost appeal.

I came here with her –
Christ, I even met her family.
Walking down these streets last night,
it all came back. Memories.

Her mother, still a looker,
her father, big and bluff, their farm
just out beyond the town. Nice people.

Comes back to me, how crazy I was for her.
I knew she felt the same.
I'd almost thought to pop the question.
It would have been the time.
I knew there was a transfer coming,
a chance for us to go together.

Then she explained she had to move back here,
that only residents could take part in the play.
So she was coming home to mum and dad.
Torn in two, but she was fixed on it.
She'd planned for twenty years, and now
her time had come.

'But Nate, you'll wait for me?'

I tried. But not too hard.

That was the end of that.

It's niggled though. I've tried for years
to find a woman who could make me feel
the way that Liesel did. Lots of women.
Some good times. Others not so good.
Some damned unpleasant bitches.
'You're just a dick on legs!' one told me
as we parted. I rather liked that phrase.
Some came close.
But never quite like Liesel.
Never close enough.

It left me with a question.
Why was it so important to her?

Why did she have to do this play?
She'd tried to tell me all about it.
Not really interested. Now I wonder.

Though having seen this place
I'm pretty sure I was well shot of her.

The others seem impressed, I'd have to say.
I'd heard them talking last night,
just a few, they might go out
walking in the morning, look around,
explore the town, perhaps the church.

Not my scene, but something still to do.

They set a quite surprising pace.
I followed. Didn't want to hold them back
and years do make a difference.
All I could do to keep them in my sights.

Lovely morning. Looked up,
saw it was a mackerel sky –
sheep cloud, they call it here.
Not good for flying, could mean
bad weather on the way.

Studying the sky,
scarcely noticed when they turned
into a little building, that it was the church.
Found myself inside before I really twigged.
At least it wasn't Catholic. No statues,
incense, stuff like that. But I'd been here
before. With Liesel and her family.

Found an empty bench right at the back.
A sit-down mightn't be a bad idea.
It's times like these I hate what aging does.

Not that I'm old. All things considered,
in good nick!

Except those stray and disconcerting moments
I'm having more and more. Reminds me
how I felt the first night when I found
I could no longer always get it up.
Covered it quite well.
Those little blue pills do the trick
when needed.

Lied to the doc.
No problems – no, all's good
in that department. He looked surprised.
'I thought that's why you'd come.'
It was – but found I couldn't bring myself
to say it. Viagra and Cialis keep me going.
Easy to find them on the web.
No need to talk about it.
It's not a problem for me.

Seemed to be a service starting.
They'd lit the candles at the front,
next a preacher walking down the aisle.
Easy to slip away, I figured,
when I got sick of it.
Meanwhile, a chance to rest.
But too much time to think.

Remember.

Caught me unawares when Cliff began
to tell me how he'd found he had a problem
in the sack department.
We've never had to worry.
Never even talked about it.
Back in those days

when we could keep it up
all night!

Flown together all these years. Met up
when we were training in the RAAF.
Then when we went commercial
tried to keep together. Christ,
must be forty years or more.
We ate together, drank together, found our way
to all the red light districts where we were.
No worries then, for either of us.

Didn't know what I should say
when now, all these years later,
he starts to tell me
how it's going wrong.
'Equipment doesn't work these days – '
That was the way he put it –
Face wretched, looking half-ashamed,
told me how it makes him feel.

Couldn't bring myself to say I understood.
Too well.

He used to look at me with envy. When he married,
settled down, he'd watch me pulling birds
without a care, and smile good-humouredly.
But Marilyn made sure he kept the crown jewels
for her use alone.

No need for that these days, he said.
Not much use in them anymore.
And not much use to her.

'I dunno, Nate. It makes me feel
I'm not a man. Not any more.
Wish that I was you. You've always
pulled them in, you lucky bastard.'

I couldn't tell him it was just the same
for me. The words just wouldn't come.

Not like me to be stuck for words.
Thought about it, sitting in this place.

Lots of singing going on around me.
Doleful German hymns.
Wonder how the others,
sitting down the front, are getting by.

We'd push the plane into the hangar,
Cliff and I. More an effort for us now,
than when we bought her, fifteen years ago.
Growing old together, Cliff and I
and Winifred. Don't ask me why
we called her that. Maybe some bird
that I was sleeping with back then.

There've been so many through these years
I really can't remember.
As for getting hitched,
came close one other time –
a girl called Rosemary,
but got cold feet
three days before the wedding,
and pulled out.
She wasn't Liesel.
Just didn't seem the same.
Must say, I did feel bad about it, but
it simply wouldn't have worked out.
Too many women out there.
Why confine myself to one?

Women and flying – they're my life.

So when our contract time was up,
I looked at Cliff; we'd always thought
we'd like to keep the past alive.
Retirement packages are healthy.
Bought the plane. Our golden handshake
to ourselves. A way to spend our time.
Relive old days.

Flying and women – they're my life!
And they've been Clifford's too,
Except for him it's just been Marilyn.
Strange that. He always played the field.
But after Marilyn that changed.
Used that old line: with steak at home,
no need to go out after hamburger.
I shrugged.
But wondered.
Still, with home meeting all his needs ….
But now,
if age was catching up with him?

'What does she say?' I asked him, curious.
Wondered how a wife reacted.

He sort of groaned. 'Hell mate.
It makes it worse. She's kind!
Wants me to see a doc.'

'You've got to, anyway. The yearly medical
is coming up. No way you can get out of that.'

We had a saying: Death, taxes, CASA.
All unavoidable.
First two were bad enough.
Yet in some ways the flying tests were worse.

Never occurred to us he wouldn't pass the medical.

That was a blow quite unforeseen.
Like saying, finished mate!
You've had your run.

I tried to rally him. 'We'll fly together.
I've got five years on you. It's going to be
the way it's always been.'

But I could see it wasn't working.
For Cliff it was another body blow.

Up there the parson's talking now. He said it
first in German, now it's English.
Gloomy stuff, a bleak black world.
Disciples in the courtyard,
a pre-dawn with the crowing rooster.
Sermons from my childhood, with my mum
at church. Easter, and the stories I recall.
Often think of Peter, and the way he felt,
when he'd let down his friend.

The friend who trusted him.
Like Cliff, with me.

We flew together, certainly, but not the same.
The whole affair had knocked the stuffing
out of him. I could understand.
This ageing is a bugger. Simple things:
days we moved the plane –
my muscles ached that night.
My glasses need to be
much stronger than they were.
I have a nasty feeling that the TV's softer
than it used to be. I guess my turn
is coming too.

I watched Cliff getting thinner, greyer,
looking at me with a sort of envy.

'You've still got it all.'
And even now I let him think that it was so.
too proud to tell him otherwise.

Would it have made a difference?

We'd spent the morning out, a clear bright day.
Could see for miles. Plane running like a dream.
Came into the canteen for some lunch.

'I want,' he looked me in the eye, 'one more flight
on my own. Last solo flight, then they can
put me on the shelf.'

'Mate, I can't let you. You know that.
You're not a licensed pilot any more.'

Not surprised.

'Knew that you'd say that. You've always been
such a self-righteous prick.
You've never had to face a problem
in your life. You've always been
the golden boy.'

Wanted to tell him how it really was.
Words wouldn't come.
So shook my head, and went off for a piss.
Stood in there for a long time,
thinking.

Like now. Thinking doesn't help.
All round me, people getting up
and filing to the front. Reminds me
when I was a little tacker, went to church
with mum, communion. She'd come back,
whiff of port around her as she bent in prayer.
What was she praying for?

What would I pray for?
If I prayed.

A chance to talk to him again, perhaps?
A chance to tell him, mate, you're not alone.

Would that have made a difference?

I knew … can't kid myself … I knew
when I came back and he was gone,
I'd missed my chance to speak.

They called the crash an accident.

But then we both knew that the old girl
wasn't worth much any more.
He might have thought insurance
was a better option.

Accident?
Perhaps it was.

Cliff gone. The Winifred as well.
I miss them both. Old days are over.
Liesel's gone, and all the others
after her. What's left for me?

Hard to look at Marilyn, grey-faced
and weeping at the funeral. Especially
when she said: 'You were such friends,
so many years. He so admired you.'

Letting down a friend. Perhaps
the worst thing you can do.
Judging by the preacher's words,
Peter thought so too.

They're standing up around me.
Must be all over.
Hip twinges as I get up, slowly.
Woman coming down the aisle
is from our group.
Thought for a minute she was smiling
at me. Then realised she'd turned
towards the man beside her.

Women don't see me anymore.
Guess that's the way it's going to be.

Caroline

Strange.
I should be feeling just so happy.
I was.
Elated. Quite ecstatic.
That call was everything I wanted.

Briefly, I was.

And then, I don't know why, something
different seemed to pass a cloud
across my happiness.

Can't quite identify it. Uneasy.

It's this place; it's these people.

Why?

No time to think about it now.

Time to join the crowds that stream
towards the Spielhaus, that vast building
where the play is staged.

Find my door and queue.

It's what we're here for, after all.

No, wait a minute.
Don't want to get caught up with him,
that foul-mouthed sexist idiot
in the line ahead.
Last night's dinner conversation
was hard enough to take.

AL: THE MILLER'S TALE

He was a Rangler and a goliardeys,
And that was most of sinne and harlotrye.
Well coulde he stelen corn, and tollen thryes …

A wrangler and buffoon, he had a store
Of tavern stories, filthy in the main.
His was a master-hand at stealing grain …

Stuck here now, so might as well
go through with it. Not my sort of show
at all. No idea what I was getting into.

Heard about Munich. Famous for the beer.
Big show, Oktoberfest. That's my style.
Saw pictures of those German birds
with mugs of beer, ten or more,
all balanced, pushing through
mobs of drinkers.
Looked the place for me.
Knew I could outdrink the best of them.

Got here months too early, had to fill in time.
Thought, might as well stay here as travel on.
Get into practice.
Found myself some mates.

Pissed one night. Loaded to the gills.

Bloke at our table had a ticket for this show
at Oberammergau. Never heard of it.
He needed cash.
Said that it was another German festival.

Suckered me.
Said it would be just like Oktoberfest –
but early.

Thought he was the real McCoy.
You don't expect another Aussie –
especially one from Vic – to shake you down!

We'd drunk together for the afternoon.
Swapped notes on how we'd fetched up
here. My football past. He was impressed
to hear my stories of the games I'd played.
Year we made Grand Final. Clubs I'd coached.

Mind you, I stretched the tales a bit.

Left out some bits I'd rather not
have passed around.

Especially with the mob I'm stuck with now.
Red hot pokers up their arses, all of them!
No wonder,
coming to this show. But by the time
I'd sussed out what it really was,
too late. I'd handed over cash
and wasn't going to see it go to waste.

Closer that today came, more I cursed
that dickhead in the pub.

Tried to find out more about it.

Music and singing, someone said next day –
led me down the garden path with that.
Never objected to a song and dance affair.
Took the missus when we were together
to some shows. Not too bad a night.
Don't think this will be like that.

From what I've heard the others say.
seems to be a churchy sort of show.

Must have had a real skinful to get conned
like this. Mug born every minute,
so they say. I must be one.
Nearer it's got,
the less I like the notion.
Almost turned it in this morning.
Don't think the others would have been surprised.

Stuffed shirts, the lot! Tight-arsed women,
bloodless looking men. A few poofs
in the group as well, I'd bet a quid or too.

Last night got stuck into the beer at dinner.
Told some stories. Thought I might lighten up
the atmosphere. Some of my best.
Might not have been the right group for them.
Went down like lead balloons.
Saw one woman, teacher-looking sort,
look at her friend, her eyebrows raised.

'What brings you here?' another prissy one
asked me outright.
'Good of my health!' I said.
That shut her up. The big guy
with the dog collar, a bishop, someone said,
came to me later. Almost human,
even if he was what grand-dad called
a sky pilot, and said he's seen me play.
(Glad I didn't tell my bishop joke last night.)
'They used to have a name for you, I think?'
he asked. 'What was it now? The stud?'

'You're close,' I told him.
Papers used to say, 'The bull.'

Name I was proud of, actually.
'Ah yes,' he said, 'I saw you play.
You took some bloody brilliant marks.
I do remember now.'

Wondered if he remembered all the rest of it.

That girl who got police involved. As if she
hadn't asked for it. The six of us
were up on charges, but clearly it was just
her word or ours. Club's lawyers
had no trouble showing her
for what she was.
She told us she was older!
Well, that was what we said.
Didn't do the club much good.
We got our warnings.

'You're not coaching any more?' he asked.

He couldn't have been keeping up with news.
All over telly and the papers when they
'let me go.' I never thought a quiet bet or two
would ever come back, bite me in the bum.
You'd think sports writers should have
more to do than muck rake like they do.
They'll always find a pot to piss in.

Good severance money, but.
They were so keen to keep it quiet.
Avoid a scandal even if it cost.
Thought that it might be time for me
to see the world.

Problem is I've always been too trusting.
They'd said those bets were on the QT.
I believed them. They were drinking mates.

Just like that bloke in Munich at the Hofbräuhaus.
I should have smelled a rat when he was willing
to give away this ticket at half price.
Only question is how someone like him
came to have an entry for this show.

Well, I've got the ticket.
Might as well go in.
Size of this crowd surprising.
Hard to find the door I have to go in by.
Must be at least a dozen ways inside.
More.
Maybe twenty entry doors.
Huge building, like a footy stadium.
Pity it's not.
And milling people pushing in.
Just like the footy –
but I'm not expecting
anything I could enjoy.

Lost the others from this tour. No one
I'd want to be with. Guess we'll be
all together somewhere in this sea of seats
and faces.

We're a group, no matter how
they feel about me.
'Rough diamond, there,'
I heard the snooping woman say. From what
I've heard way back in Sunday school
(yes, for a year or two mum made me go)
this Jesus used to have rough diamonds
in his team, and didn't turn a hair.

Caroline

I knew that it was big –
but this is vast,
more like a football stadium
than theatre.

I find my way past stalls and booths,
piles of cushions, rugs for rent,
small torches for the night to come,
enabling us to read the script,
guide books, librettos – multi-lingual,
like the crowds who now flock in.

Inside the auditorium hum of noise,
five thousand voices murmuring,
sound echoes through this caverned space.
Anticipation rises.

Our seats, two rows, are good –
I check. Our group's all here,
though Luke, the mohawked picture
of rebellious youth, is clearly most unhappy
to find his seat is next to dad.
He hunches well away, rejects
all conversation and the offered script.

It's time. The gathering subsides
and noise is stilled.
'About to start ...' the man beside me
states the obvious. But then,
high churchmen are well-known for that.

I wonder what he brings to this.
His presence here ... an act of faith?

Or, as John has suggested,
an extra gloss to his credentials
for a step upwards in the hierarchy?

My musing stops.
The white-robed figures of the chorus
file in from either side.

I shiver, as I feel
an unexpected prickle of anticipation.

The man beside me straightens up,
alert he waits.

JUSTIN: THE MONK'S TALE

A manly man, to be an abbot able …
What sholde he studie, and make him-selven wood,
Upon a book in cloistre alwey to poure,
Or swinken with his handes, and laboure …?

A manly man, to be an Abbot able …
What! Study until reason lost dominion
Poring on books in cloisters? Must he toil
As Austin bade and till the very soil?

A good procession at the start.
Always a good sign. Those opening notes,
the trumpet's sound, and then the robed choir
files in from the wings, and takes position
in the forefront of the open stage.
Impressive.
They've changed the costumes since last time.
No surprise. Ten years have passed.
Must keep it up to date.

Clear day today. Fortunate.
That stage exposed to elements is risky.
The last time I was here it drizzled
intermittently.
All very well for us, the audience.
They roofed the viewers' area
some decades back. Performers though –
another matter. They soldiered on.
They always do, in rain or shine.

Commitment.
Rare in this age.

Close on four hundred years to keep
this Passion Play alive. Amazing.

My third time here. I think it lends
a credibility to my religious life.
I mention it in all the places where it counts.
They look at me with interest.
A man to watch.

Most important now, this year. I need
to make it clear to everyone I am the one,
the one to lead our church through times
we all foresee as challenging.

A good word that. Sounds suitable,
Church militant. That's what we need to be.

As straight performance this year's play
is interesting. New young director.
Fresh ideas. Not sure I like them all.

Past decades were all day performances;
a morning through to evening affair.
This year it's bells and whistles;
noon to night, and fireworks, they say.
Lightning flashes when the death scene comes.

The crucifixion, if you will.
So many find that word too ugly; I feel
we must not terrify our people with
images of blood and torture.
Congregations don't want that from church.

Choir's good this year. It's stirring.
Woman next to me is wiping tears away.
It's got to her. Impressive that this little town
can keep it going, every decade. All of them,
performers, singers, players, from these parts.
What a tradition.

Traditions keep the church alive. Without
the rituals, the ceremonies, we wouldn't last.
Amazing though, how all those happy-clappy sects
can get the people in.
Never understand it.
Our numbers falling,
while the sects are growing.
Strange.

Now watch this lot on stage.
Jerusalem, and there you have it all.
Procession with a crowd.
What are they doing?
Strewing branches of the palm trees
down in front of him,
even though he's on a donkey.
Calling Hallelujahs –
that's exactly what I mean.
People like a show.

Bring on their leaders, and you see the same.
Those costumes. They're quite splendid.
(Must cost a fortune to outfit this play.
I've read the silks come straight from India.)
Much finer than our leaders ever wear.

Yet I've heard criticisms – not direct to me,
you understand – but that some people say
our bishop's robes are far too grand.
Money better spent on feeding those
in poverty and hunger. 'Feed my sheep!'

That won't stop me wearing bishop's robes
with pride next year when I'm appointed.
There's good foundation, furthermore.
'The poor,' Christ said it to the twelve,
'you'll always have with you.'

'I'm not, of course, suggesting we don't help.
That's quite opposed to what we stand for.
But careful choices – they are what we need.

Just look at him on stage – old Caiaphas.
That robe, that headgear.
You need to look like that.
It's honouring God.
Shows that you're paying him respect.
Others see it that way too.
Church leaders need to be impressive.

It's one of my real assets. I look the part.

It won't be quite clear-cut, I know.
There's others think they're in there
with a chance. I could name names.
But won't. Undiplomatic. Dangerous.

We all know who I mean. There's one
who thinks his extra years of study,
list of degrees, make him prime candidate.
He simply doesn't realise
it's not just what you know, but who,
that gets a man ahead these days.
Yes, even in the church. I've never
been a one for study. Good first degree,
but not much time in books
after those days. Far more important
to get on boards, committees,
build your network, lots of contacts.
I spend my evening hours at meetings,
not with my head in books.

Then there's another
who lives in ostentatious poverty,
and thinks that this will bring him honours.

He little understands that making those of us
who like a good meal and a glass or two
of wine – and good wine only – feel guilty,
won't make him any friends.
More a reproach.
No one likes that.

To get on in the church you need to play the game.
Know just who's in, who's out,
in thinking of the powers that be.

Those two on stage,
Annas and Caiaphas, the Jewish leaders,
they understood.
They knew they had to play along
with Rome. They knew the way
to get exactly what they wanted.
We see them handle Pilate,
the skill with which they play on
all his fears … impressive.
You watch and see.
You can learn quite a lot from them.
Not for good ends, of course.
I must make that quite clear.

You have to learn to separate the means from ends.
But sometimes rather doubtful means
are needed to achieve one's ends.
I don't condone – how could I? –
what they were about.
That would be unforgivable.

But watch the cleverness
with which they did it.

Didn't Christ himself point out to followers
that they should learn the methods of the sinful world?

That parable he told about the wicked servant
who saw dismissal coming and made friends
out of his master's debtors … good model there!

That clinches it for me.

I've made my friends, both in and out the church.
I've kept my nose clean, all the way.
Some tricky times I've weathered.
A few I look back on uneasily, I must admit.

Those moments in the middle of the night,
when you remember things
the daylight hours blot out.

Just sometimes when a scandal loomed,
I've managed to side-step quite neatly.
Kept the church's name, and mine,
out of the gutter press. Things happen
that breed doubt. It's better to leave faith
serene, untroubled.

We've shifted people round a bit,
I will confess, when rumours proved
too strong to quite ignore. There's times
when I have felt uneasy, watching what went on.

Cases referred to me I've managed to steer
clear of. Floated on above the murk, and left
the public side in others' hands.
Just pushed the raft from underneath.
Suggestions how things might be handled.
'Move him elsewhere.'
Always a good line. You never know.

It surely is our job to give the sinner
chances to repent, amend his ways.

Yet always when the moment comes
when I watch how they managed it,
uneasy.

Those thirty silver pieces handed over
to Judas by the Jewish leaders, I wonder
just how many meetings I've sat in,
voted how to handle difficult affairs,
in ways that sometimes in bad nights
can make me toss and turn.

But then the church must be protected.

In their misguided way – I emphasise
'misguided' – don't get me wrong! I'm not
condoning what they did – those leaders
tried to keep safe what they had.
We all know crowds can be manipulated.
They managed that alright.

The same way we manipulate?

It's the responsibility of those with power
to work for what is best.
Best for whom?
A troubling question.

I don't read much, but every now and then
I look again at that old work on power,
Machiavelli's *Prince*.
He understood the problems of the man in charge.

If Caiaphas and Annas got it wrong –
I don't mean 'if' – of course they did – but
I can empathise with them, and the dilemma
that they found they had.

My third time here at Oberammergau.

First time, three decades back, I wonder
if I thought this way?
Callow youth, fresh from my ordination,
why did I come?
An act of dedication? And commitment?

Or was it that already I could sense
that I was destined for big things?
For thirty years the church has groomed me
for the role. And taught me skills I need.

But were there things
that eager boy once knew
that I have now forgotten?

A foolish speculation. This trip
consolidates my place. And when next year
the choice falls on me, as it surely will
(the powers that be have told me)
I'll don the robes, almost as splendid
as the ones on stage, and —
like the men who wear those —
make decisions that are needed.

Caroline

Embarrassing!

I'm really not a sentimental type.
But when I heard that opening chorus,
the swelling orchestra, the sudden sense
that for four hundred years – and more –
so many others just like me
have sat and listened to this call
to worship, it got to me.

I found myself in tears.

A sense of ages past, of insignificance
of any one of us, of any single person.

The man beside me glanced,
and then, well-bred, ignored my tears.

Women cry . . .
The softer sex.
I knew what he was thinking.

Not all of us, though.

There, on my other side, a woman
who won't cry, I'm sure of that.
They tell me that she has a reputation –
tough cookie – in the business world.

She's one of our new breed,
the women who can out-smart
all the competition of the males
she must contend with in the world.

But then, I'd thought that I was
one of these. It's what I've tried to be.

Perhaps I haven't known myself
as well as I had thought?

Does she?

MARTINE:
THE MANCIPLE'S TALE

Algate he wayted so in his achat,
That he was ay biforn and in good stat.
Now is that nat of God a ful fair grace
That swich a lewed mannes wit shal pace
The wisdom of an heep of lerned men?

He used to watch the market most precisely
And got in first, and so he did quite nicely.
Now isn't it a marvel of God's grace
That an illiterate fellow can outpace
The wisdom of a heap of learned men?

They talk about me as the woman
with the golden touch.
Term used in newspapers,
the year I won awards –
my favourite one was
Businesswoman of the Year.
Interviews were focused on the way
I'd single-handed turned two companies around.
Then walked away.

The feature article they ran was good.
Photograph – well, touched up very slightly.
I'd dressed with care.
I understand just how important image is.

My change of job? The interviewer probed.
Why had I moved? And such a move.
Replace the world of commerce with religion?

I smiled, and answered crisply.
'A new challenge!'

Unusual, they said. A woman CEO,
Business administrator of a church.
Weren't there glass ceilings in this world
where males had dominated for so many years?

Years? How I smiled inside.
Decades. Centuries. A truer estimate.
But kept my face serene, composed.

'The church has always been prepared
to open paths for women.'
Went on to quote those characters
from early days, the Lydias, the Annas,
Marys too, the ones we cite
to demonstrate how just and fair and honest
in dealing with our sex the church has been.

You couldn't blame the journalist
for looking cynical. She knew
as well as I the lie this was.
The centuries when women were reduced
to ciphers, suited only to supporting roles.

Don't get me started on it.

I'm not a feminist in spite of how I feel.

'Lucky?' she asked. 'Have you been lucky
to get on and rise the way you have?'

We make our luck ourselves. We learn
to play the game as men have played it
all these years. Take opportunities that come.
Seize the advantage when we see it.
Use every asset we can find.

No place for softness and do-gooder attitudes.
This is a cut-throat world.
If you are not prepared to wield the knife,
then stay at home and nurture children.

I made my choice, and there are no regrets.

But still, I had the wit to look demure
before the panel of old men
who put me through my paces in the interview.
My CV was impeccable – that I knew.
Background experience no one could fault.
Degrees far in advance of all
the other candidates (I'd checked them out.)

But still, the disadvantage.
I was female.
So I deferred, and flattered.
Took advice on issues
where my knowledge far exceeded theirs.
Glass ceilings may not shatter,
but can be penetrated –
with sufficient care.

For their church was in trouble, and they knew it.
An institution of the past, unlikely to survive
the challenges of a new age. They needed me.

Essential to bring business practices into
this world of milksop kindness, charity to all.
No way to run a company.

I took my time to see how things were done.
Weighed up the situation, saw the waste.
Then when the time was right, began
to wield the pruning knife. Or shears.

A leaner keener institution, I told them.

'And meaner ...' Oh yes, I heard
the mutters in the corridors of power.
So when jobs went and roles were re-defined,
and ancient hangers-on were pastured out,
they saw that times had changed.

Budget cuts and new priorities.
The church, like any business institution,
must run efficiently.
Adopt commercial practices,
learn from the world outside these cloistered walls.
'You brought me here,'
I told them when I saw raised brows,
'because you knew disaster loomed.
You need sound business principles.'

Ignored the murmurs of distress
and *sotto voce* talk of 'other principles'
as they watched cuts, redundancies,
and cherished projects scrapped.

Uneasily they watched and worried over
my investment program.
'It seems,' said one old innocent, 'too much
like gambling.' While others were concerned
about the ethics of the companies
that we were now involved with.
You don't look closely at the morals
of your stock market choices;
factors like the profit margin
count far more.

Of course I didn't say that to them.

Tough times need tough decisions.
I'm used to these – you might say
they're my stock in trade.

I doubt they knew when they appointed me
my last board called me 'hatchet woman.'
Behind my back, of course.

Cuts must be made. It's only sense
to find the units that are not achieving
and cost most. The Rehab Centre
and the Street Kids program –
costly, inefficient.
Few results from these.

I've left them with the facts and figures.
When I return, they will have seen
the truth of what I say.
They have to go.

As for the Meditation Centre, soup kitchens,
prayer stations in the city streets at Easter time …
It's money down the drain.
The few who come to faith through these
must learn the church is not a charity.

'A bankrupt church can do no good
for anyone!' I pointed out to critics.
They talked about the great god Mammon
whom, they thought, I worshipped.

No wonder that it comes to mind right now.
The curtains open on the stage
and there it is, another frozen scene,
a 'living image', or *tableau vivant;*
these are the names my Passion Play guide book
gives to these scenes.
Old Testament tales … They're interspersed
between scenes of the Passion story,
like pictures in the old-time Children's Bibles.

This tableau, I could swear, is taken
quite directly from a book I can recall.
I was an earnest child, absorbed.
Its illustrations were like scenes on stage.
A simple faith, that child's.
A pity that those days,
that faith, soon passes.

It's Moses and the Golden Calf,
with all the crowds bowed down in worship
in defiance of his censure.

The image that for centuries has been
embodiment of avarice, cupidity, and –
to its critics – corporate greed.
Meanwhile, in front of stage,
the Chorus sings the story of this scene
and earlier days.

The curtains close; the Chorus singers file away.
Now the play resumes its presentation
of the events of Holy Week. Act Three,
with eight more still to stage. I sigh,
and contemplate again my motives.
What led me to come here?

Worth looking at, I'd thought. A trip
to Oberammergau would be a good finale,
a fitting ending to my investigation.
Central business offices,
discussions with administrators
of partner churches overseas in lands
that faced a similar raft of problems.

Our church is not alone.
In every place I visited, the same.

Numbers falling, income down,
expenses higher. A world-wide picture.

How do the others cope?
What can we learn? And what avoid?
I kept it brief, selected countries carefully.
Fact-finding mission, so I called it
in my application. Or research.
That word they understood.

But looked dismayed, those grey old men,
and wondered at the costs. They recognised
my value, knew how unwise it would be
to demur. I have an instinct. I can see
potential. Why else would I be here?

It's not a junket, tacked on to my trip.

This Passion Play, that draws so many,
a half a million people to a little village,
is affirmation to the world
that churches still have power. But more,
a money-maker if ever I have seen one –
there must be some way we can build on this.
It needs thought.

The Tableau Vivant over, we're back
in Christ's Jerusalem, main players
on the stage again. This time a temple scene.
The milling crowds of Jews, and Jesus comes
to worship, his disciples clustering close.

The stage is crowded, bustling jostling people
of all ages. They say two thousand
of the village are involved when each ten years
this spectacle is staged. For it's spectacular indeed!

A good percentage must be in this scene right now.
Small children, animals, old men, young women
with their babes, Jewish leaders, merchants,
traders on the temple steps, and in the forecourt
a thriving scene of commerce, as worshippers
make purchases, to offer as their sacrifice.

Travellers from near and far have come
to worship in this most sacred place,
the Jewish temple, for it's Passover.
The money changers now provide
the needed Temple coinage – I'm sure
their rates are profitable. This is
a booming centre of church life.

But as we watch we see
how Christ strides forward,
grasps a trader's whip,
and lays about him.

A scene of vast confusion – tables overturned,
the coins are scattered on the ground
and children scrabble for their share.
The oil vats are upended and the floor's awash.
The panicked animals run wild; the sheep and goats
resist recapture by their furious owners;
the doves fly heavenward; hens screech
and squawk and flutter out of reach.

And overall the voice of Jesus comes,
in righteous fury. I check my copy
of the text to find translation of his words.

'A house of prayer,' he says,
'but in your hands
a den of thieves.'

He turns attack upon the priests, the ones
who should have been the guardians of the place.
'Abomination – and you tolerate it!'
His words of accusation ring across the vastness
of the audience; on stage his hearers quiver.

'Is this God's house?' he asks.
'Or just a market-place?'
'How can the people worship God in this?'

I watch the stage, but my eyes go to Judas,
where he stands aghast, as coins are flung
and fought for. I see him thinking 'Waste!'

I can relate.

Just as I felt for Judas, and indeed, with him,
when in an earlier scene his was the voice
that remonstrated, for Mary Magdalene
had poured expensive perfume
over Jesus' feet.
Waste!

'It could have been so profitably sold;
the money used for some good purpose,'
he upbraided them.

No comfort in Christ's words.
'Why do you criticise what's done for love?'

But I could see the point that Judas made:
'It's my responsibility,' he pointed out,
'to manage money for our group ...'

I knew exactly how he felt. It's very well
for visionaries and philosophers to take
a line like this, but those of us who live
in the real world know that one must be
practical!

But then, it's Judas who betrays his Lord –
his final choice of practical over ideal?
I wonder if I'll feel the same
when that scene comes.

I'll think about that later. For now,
the Passion Play continues.

The Chorus is returning, and the curtains
open on another tableau scene. Again,
Old Testament. Now we're in Egypt:
it's the night before they leave.
Families eat the first Passover meal.

In watching this
I can obliterate the vague unease
created by Christ's action in the Temple.
It can be blotted out.
For now.

Caroline

First half over, and it's dinner break.

The crowds disgorge. Hunger calls
and, purposeful, we make our way
to allocated restaurants.

Some thoughtful, meditating on
what's passed. Most simply focused
on the need to get there fast,
present their dinner vouchers, eat.

I walk among them, still unseeing,
immersed in stage and music.
This Passion Play,
for all I'd known about it,
has caught me by surprise.
The scope, the grandeur, the intensity,
these things were not what I'd expected.

We take our places at the table,
amid the clatter of the dining crowds.
I look at others, wonder if they too
have been surprised.

Near me our master chef appraises
dishes as they come, a quiet scrutiny,
for, opposite, accustomed to an audience,
the barrister holds forth.

TOM: THE MAN OF LAWE'S TALE

In termes hadde he caas and domes alle,
That from the tyme of king William were falle
Therto he coulde endyte, and make a thing,
Ther coulde no wight pinche at his writing
And every statut coulde he pleyn by rote.

❦

He knew of every judgement, case and crime
Recorded ever since King William's time.
He could dictate defences or draft deeds;
No one could pinch a comma from his screeds,
And he knew every statute off by rote.

You say it's not just what you know,
but who, that counts.
I'd challenge that.

Not in my field.
You obviously know that I'm a lawyer –
a damned good one, at that.
For me, connections don't win cases;
it's knowledge of the law.

I wonder just how many of you,
sitting round this table in the dinner break,
have seen a courtroom at close quarters.
If you were in trouble, how you'd choose
the man for your defence. A lawyer
who was well-connected, or the one
who knew his stuff.

Just look around this room, this restaurant,
the *Ammergauerhaus*. How many would you say

it holds? Come on, let's hazard
a guess here. Two hundred? Maybe more.

These stolid Germans and the foreigners, like us,
slurping down *Tomatensuppe* –
so you selected *Pfannenkuchensuppe*, did you? –
do you think they'd prefer to face the court
with someone who was well-connected,
networked well,
or someone who could get them off?

For that's my specialty. I get them off.

I think you all know who I am.
My name's well-publicised. And certainly
the recent cases have had coverage
in daily news that's made me
more of a public figure than
I might have chosen.

Notorious?

An unkind word. I'll grant you that
some of my cases may have been
a little on the seamy side, to put it mildly.

People tend to hear my name, and then
pre-judge the issue. Must be a criminal,
if Tom Gillooley's taking the defence.

I know I am first port of call
in any dubious affair.

And many a man has, beaming,
joined me on the courthouse steps,
smiling for the cameras, free to go,
where not so skilled an advocate might well
have left him on the primrose path

to prison. My client list may truly be
an underworld who's who. So what?

You think I should refuse such cases?

That attitude, these moral scruples,
are based on false assumptions.
In fact, they prejudge issues.
If we assume, and so we must,
that men are innocent
until the courts determine guilt –
the basis of our legal system –
how can you justify refusal
of a proper legal representative
to anyone, no matter who?

Someone has to do it.
It must be done whole-heartedly,
the best case that it's possible to make.

My job. I'm good at it.

It's not my role to prejudge issues.
It's my responsibility to find the version
most favourable to the accused.
Then leave it to the judge
and jury to decide.

It's better not to know too much.
I never ask them: 'Innocent or guilty?'
I must be free to put the best case
that I can.

You, sir, you're looking horrified.
You are a churchman, and you think
there's no defence for sin.
Guilt must be punished.

Ah, but first
the guilt must be determined, sir!

You think I should be seeking truth.
A slippery concept, that.
In fact, your Jesus made it very clear
when Pontius Pilate asked the question:
'What is truth?'

He had no answer.

So I defend them all, and ask no questions.
Decisions are the jury's job, not mine.

And if I know the answer, in my heart,
I blot it out. My job is to defend,
not prosecute. This is the role
I've chosen. All my years
of learning are devoted to that end.

I rarely lose a case.
That is the reason that they come to me.
They know they're in good hands.
The best.

I can command the fees I want,
and have the lifestyle I enjoy.
The luxuries that make life good,
the travel that has taken me
from land to land, and even brought me
here – a sudden whim, but one
I don't regret. If Christ had had me
as defending counsel, the story
would have ended very differently!

I can manipulate events,
show new perspectives on the evidence,
find counter-witnesses and precedents.
Then bring about the outcome that we want.

Not always popular, of course.

But now I think I'll leave you to your meal.
The fish was good, but coffee here is dodgy.
I'll see you all back at the Spielhaus,
when evening presentation of the play
resumes. The dinner break still leaves me
time to walk a little round the town.

◌

But walking leads to thought.

Better avoided.

I don't regret it, any of it.
I made my choices
and I'll stick with them.
But when I said to them,
My fellow diners in the restaurant,
that outcomes of my cases often weren't
too popular, it barely touched reality.

Too many scenes live in my mind.

Bitter tears of families when a driver
walks away, doubt cast upon
his drunkenness,
a widow and her children left bereft.

Fathers who wait for me,
threatening violence, when the man
charged with their daughter's rape
goes free.

The mobster who treats me as bosom friend,
refers me to his friends, establishes
a clientele who pay my bills, using money
that I'd rather not know much about.

The death threats – yes, I've had these –
when a witness suddenly goes missing,
or unaccountably forgets what he
had claimed to see.
I don't ask questions.

My daughter does though. Sometimes
I wonder if her mother sets up an agenda.
Weekends that Lily comes to me
she asks what I am working on.
I see the silent criticism in her eyes.
Just like her mother's used to be,
until she went her way.
Easier for us both.

The last case Lily questioned closely.

They'd managed to get extradition
of two directors who had fled
the country after failure of their companies.
Of course they came to me.
Courtroom packed audiences every day.
Crowds of retirees looking angry
and baby boomers who had lost a packet
when the deal turned sour.

They should have realised
the estimated profits sounded warning bells.
But people are so greedy.
Then think they can complain
when things go wrong.

Mind you, those two were dubious!
Quite plausible, it's true. But still,
you'd be a fool to sink your whole life savings
with them. Yet many did.

I got them off, of course.
Made it quite clear
that any criminal activity
was further down the line.
Their hands were clean.

It didn't help when two weeks later
the police found John and Mara White
together in their car,
a suicide pact outcome from their losses,
and newspapers were quick to draw connections.

So was my daughter. 'Wasn't that case
one you were involved in, Dad?' she asked.
'However could you defend men like that?
Our Civics teacher said
the verdict was disgraceful!'

'My job!' I told her smartly.
'Like anyone who's charged,
they have a right to be defended.
And Lily, don't forget
it's my work keeps you clothed
and at that school.'

It seemed a good time to be travelling for a while.

The young are quick to judge. I do my job
with every ounce of skill that I possess.
That doesn't call for all that holier-than-thou
from her.

When I've done my part, I wash my hands
of it; the next stage is the jury's.
not my responsibility.

Washing hands … yes, that was Pilate too.
I wait that moment in the Passion Play.

A fellow feeling. I've washed mine,
more times than him. Same feeling though.
Not my responsibility.
My hands are clean.

Sometimes it's harder though.
It's better not to look into their eyes.
I did it once,
and knew that he was guilty,
so shut my mind to it.
Worked hard, convinced the jury
there was reasonable doubt
that he had been the one
who raped the boys.
Evidence?
Circumstantial only.

But I knew.

So when, some months of freedom later,
the body of another lad was found,
I also knew that this time
I should share the guilt.

Sometimes no matter
how much hands are washed,
the smell of blood remains.
Like Macbeth's wife,
I still see spots
that nothing will clean off.

The crowds are moving back.
It's time.
The second half will start quite soon.

So now I'll go back in and watch,
especially for that moment,

when Pilate calls for servants
to bring him the bowl of water,
and he washes hands –
his cleansing from all blame.

I'll watch his face,
and see if he feels clean.

I don't.

Caroline

I saw him walking back, ahead of me,
alone.

A minister, John told me, but he didn't know
what church. I've had no chance
to talk to him.

This would have been a time.

I could quite easily have reached him,
but something in the way he looked,
the way he walked,
stopped me.

If ever I have seen sheer naked misery
upon a face, it's his.

I would have thought this presentation
should be his meat and drink,
not cause for such a look.

I can't intrude on that.

Perhaps tomorrow.
When this Passion Play is over.

ADAM: THE PARSON'S TALE

A good man was ther of religioun,
And was a povre Persoun of a toun;
But riche he was of holy thoght and werk . . .
This noble ensample to his sheep he yaf,
That first he wroghte, and afterwards he taughte.

୭୭

A holy-minded man of good renown
There was, and poor, the parson to a town,
Yet he was rich in holy thought and work . . .
This noble example to his sheep he gave,
First following the word before he taught it.

Should not have come.

Should not have come.

On train tracks in my mind
words keep spinning.
Round and round they go.

Should not have come.

What did I think I'd find?
Some magic answer from on high.
Some word from a divinity
who has left this empty shell.

My words these days are tinkling cymbals,
sounding brass –
Paul's warning newly understood.

How can I do God's will,
how preach his word,

when all within me says
he's gone from me?

I watch this Passion Play unfold,
glance sideways at the others,
faces intent. It does not matter
why they're here. Some cynical,
some curious, cautious or devoted,
they are absorbed in drama of the moment.

How could they know the anguish
this play holds for me? Its words
scar memories of what was once
the life blood of my being.
No more.

I can no longer sense the presence
of the God who once walked close to me.
All that remains is emptiness, despair.

When did it go from me?
When did he leave me?
Or did I leave him?

I am become the dry bones of the prophet.

Cast me not away from thy presence,
and take not thy holy spirit from me.

Hard to sit here, watching.
Such old familiar territory.
Those stories in the tableaux –
imbibed in childhood,
studied in my seminary years,
for decades drawn on in my sermons.

No more.
How can I preach again?

Those scenes on stage.
Expulsion from the garden –
how well I understand how they would feel,
driven out of Paradise.
Banished by the God who'd walked with them
in evening dusk.
No more that closeness.

When did I lose his presence?

Was it the slow attrition of the years?
Years when I called on him,
begged his mercy for the sufferers
in my flock – and found no answer.
Only silence.

I loved the people in my care,
and they, I think, loved me.
That image of the shepherd.
Old-fashioned, yes, but somewhere
deep inside, it was the way I felt.

I was their shepherd, they my sheep.

I tried, my God, how hard I tried
to be the carer of their souls,
the priest I was appointed.

But that familiar God whom I had known
no longer stands beside me.

No cataclysmic moment.
No sudden revelations.
No light bulb suddenly extinguished.

But just slow ebbing of the certainty
of God's expected intervention.
Near imperceptible, the distancing.

No more the warmth and comfort
I'd always felt, that he was close to me.

The creeping worm of doubt, invisible.
Not flying in the night, the howling storm,
but yet insidious. A sense of hollow emptiness
is all that's left.

Yet still I spoke the ritual words
above the bread, the wine,
and offered them
to those who knelt before me.
But where the certainty that what I held
was what the words had promised —
body, blood?
His presence gone, it was a bleak façade.

How could I deal with doubts and miseries
my people brought to me?
The emptiness of words.
'Trust and rely on Him.
He will bring comfort.'

It seemed to satisfy the hearers.
But what of me?
What peace was there for me?

I watch Job and his so-called comforters.
The tableau with its frozen figures,
the chorus sings of Job, who in the midst
of direst miseries, still trusts his God.

Curse God, and die, they urge on him.
I think again, recall the doubts
of early years. A world so filled
with miseries, disasters,
floods and famines, starvation, wars,
the blind injustices.

So where, the mockers asked,
where is your God in this?

Yet somehow even as I wrestled
with their questions, with my questions,
I stayed sure of God's presence in my life.

No more.

How can I be his priest when I no longer
feel that he is here?

'You're not alone,' my bishop's words.
'It's not uncommon for a minister to find,
exhausted with the burdens that he bears,
a crisis in his faith.
Be patient, Adam, wait.'

I waited, and abandoned hope.
The God I knew had gone from me.

'Breakdown,' they called it.
A term more accurate than I suspect they knew.
For everything that held my life together,
everything that made me what I am,
has gone. Collapsed.
I see myself – a broken man.

No quick decisions, they all urged on me.
Take time, take leave of absence.
You are exhausted. Travel. Rest.

The wife who urged this trip knew
how much I had always wanted it.
But now I'm here it's dust and ashes:
it mocks the faith I had.

What's left when god has gone?

Tormented, I have searched.
Acknowledged all my sins,
'Omission and commission' – so it goes.
I search the past, and see
years of devotion to a Lord I loved.
Back then.

I served the Lord I worshipped,
I and my family both.
I tried to walk the paths of righteousness.
I tried to do his will.

I never asked of any man
an act, a choice, an offering
I would not make myself.
To bring my people close to God.
To mirror God's love to them.
All I ever wanted.

I search my soul.
'Oh cleanse me, Lord, from secret faults …' –
my daily prayer.
'Guard me against self-righteousness.'
The prayer of every preacher,
every man of God.
'Make me a doer of thy will,
and not a speaker only.'
'Take not your holy presence from me.'

Unthinkable, this desolation. For I have
walked close to the Lord,
and known his loving presence.
Unbearable, to face such loss.

I speak to him, and no one answers.
Emptiness and desolation.
Cast off. Alone.

But not the only one. For there,
as darkness falls upon the stage,
the last scenes roll inexorably on.

I see the Christ whom I have served,
have loved,
is now betrayed, rejected, scorned.
By me. By them.
Stripped of all dignity, humiliated,
mocked and spat upon.
A victim,
yet enduring all.

Enduring?
He suffers so,
yet with a calm I cannot understand.

How can he bear these losses,
still look forgiveness at accusers,
heal the ear that Peter, his misguided friend,
cuts off when soldiers come
to take him in the garden?
Peter, who flees, deserts his master.
As do they all.

No one should face such miseries.
His patience a reproach to me.
Incomprehensible, endurance such as this.
But still he calls on God, as father;
in this, he finds his peace.

I can't feel pity, but a sense of separation.
This is not suffering as I know it.

Beside me sits a woman, one of us,
her hand to mouth, flinching
as nails are driven through the hands,
the feet.

The audience is hushed and still.
There is no sound as massively,
portentously,
the cross is raised aloft.

Determinedly I wonder
how his figure is supported there.
It's quite a feat of skill,
a presentation of this sort.
Best to consider it theatrically —
logistics of the situation.

Should not have come.

Should not have come.

But now, despite myself, I see
that figure. Blood-streaked.
Blood-stained.
Tormented twisted body.

Yet he can beg forgiveness for his killers.
'They know not what they do.'

He hangs there, suffering,
the two thieves by his side.
Still he cares for others.
For them, and for his mother.

There's nothing there for me.

Until the cry of agony is heard,
the cry that rises in my throat.
I hear the words that I too call, each day,
each night, from deep inside.
The crowds who listen do not understand.
I do.

Eloi! Eloi!
Lama sabachtani!

My God! My God!
Why have you forsaken me!

I hear and know
that this is for him too
the greatest torment there can be.
Abandonment by God.

He suffered and endured this
black night of the soul.
At last I share his pain.
I know that he shares mine.

So now at last I weep;
I know he understands.

In weeping find
a life still to be lived,
a possibility of peace,
a promise of return.

I pray the psalmist's prayer.

Restore to me the joy of thy salvation;
and uphold me with thy free spirit.

In this I trust.

Caroline

I think about the way we left the play
each in our silent worlds
enclosed and separate.

The resurrection scene, so brief.
so cryptic as an ending.
An affirmation, yes.
But one quick scene, then finished.

The final choruses.
Last Hallelujahs.
Triumphant affirmation.

Suddenly it's over,
This long day's at an end.
Foreshadowing of other ends, perhaps.

I watched them as they left the playhouse.
Wondered, as they went,
how each might feel.

These travellers; my task. So much
I've learned about each one.
But yet, I know so little.
For while they've talked to me,
have told me something of their lives,
I know there's so much more.
Unspoken. Unrevealed.

If I could get inside their minds
and feel what they are feeling . . .
Insight. Not just empathy.
I wonder what I'd find.

Not hard, with some.
I hear the five, my 'good old boys',
who dozed a little
in the row in front of me;
a good few beers at dinner
helped them through the night.

Until the crashing thunder and the piercing lights
that followed on the crucifixion scene –
these woke them from their slumbers.

They'd told me they had only come
'to humour their mate Len' –
he, at least, seemed to have found
the play absorbing. Now he walks
a bit apart, as I suspect he always is.

We set off back to our hotel,
through dark streets,
warmth of summer night,
crowds quiet now,
no more the chatter of the entry,
exhausted by the hours we have lived through.

Doug, walking close to Karen,
slips his arm around her waist.
She turns to him, and smiles.
There is togetherness, and there is peace.
'I've come to a decision ... I'll fight on.'
She nods. 'I'd hoped you would.
You have too much to give to run away.'

He ponders. 'I want to feel
that I still can do some good somewhere.
Flight is the coward's way.

Not mine.
It doesn't give our son
the message that we'd want to offer.'
She smiles to hear the words 'our son'
although both know
the boy has not returned from dinner break
to join them in the playhouse.
They see ahead a long hard road,
but know now that
they travel it together.

Another pair who walk more closely
than they did.
My friend the wine merchant
who talked to me of crops and vintages,
but told me nothing of himself,
save that this trip had been
his dead wife's planning.
His sombre face had shown me
that this was important.
But yet I see him
smile warmly at the woman
by his side, and she and he seem now
to walk in step.
Two histories to put aside.
Another single road ahead to share.

Not so for all.
I see that Elinor remains aloof,
detached, still on the outskirts of our group,
a cloak of solitude about her.
Her grief is palpable and raw.
We know the story
of her friend who died,
why now she's here alone.

It's almost possible to feel her lamentation.
We cannot know
the words that she would never share.

Kitty, how I failed you. We owe each other
kindness, care. I failed you in compassion.
That moment in the play when he, the Christ,
in agony looks from the cross but sees
his mother's need, and tells the friend he loves
to take her in his care. How could I so
abandon you? Too late. My life came first.
One day there might have been some time for you.
The play gives promise of forgiveness,
even to those whose penitence comes late.
I saw the dying thief, the choice he made.
All I can do is pray for me it's not too late.
Too late.

'Too late.'
Two words she spoke aloud, and with such misery.
I would have gone to join her,
but the other got there first.
The younger woman, Linda,
the winner of the cooking contest.
A closed book, that one.
Talked to me about the competition,
but told me nothing of herself.
Her grandmother, she said.
This trip had been her dearest wish.
She'd chosen it in memory of her,
a sort of thank you
for her years of care.

But now I see her go to Elinor,
and touch her arm.
A look of such intensity.
She seems to question.
Again the words hang silent in the night.

Too late? I heard you say these words.
They're on my mind. Will I regret it,
hate myself, if I remain aloof,
resist her pleas,
procrastinate, stay hard of heart,
until it is too late?
In spite of all, she is my mother.
Time to forgive?
Perhaps, even, forget?

The older woman nods her head,
and they begin to talk.
It's not for me, a private conversation.
Elinor and Linda,
there's more to both their stories, clearly,
than they've let me know.

Presumption on my part!
Delusion! That they'd unpack
the baggage they have brought to Oberammergau
with me!

But how I wish I knew
what they are taking from here.

And what of me?

Tonight can I expect
another call from Rob?
Now that this trip is almost over?

Last night his voice, his *Cara mia*
stirred my heart with all the past,
the old familiar ache of love.
But now I start to wonder.
is the price too high?

DAY 4 and 5

AFTERWARDS

Oberammergau
– Munich
– Singapore

Caroline – return to Munich

Strangely subdued, we sit at breakfast.
The conversation casual, each locked
in our own thoughts.

It's aftermath. Wind down.
The sense of something we have shared,
if tenuous, these filament connections.
Surprising, though, that spider webs are strong.

Our tour guide, earnest anxious Irmgard,
comes to rally, organise, checks that we've
followed orders. All our luggage ready
at our doors. The bus will soon be loaded.

Please to meet her promptly for departure.

Evaluation forms. She hands them out,
explaining that her company requires
this feedback. If we would be so good
as to complete it on the bus, return it to her
at the end of journey.

On board, we spread ourselves and take advantage
of the space for privacy. Accept her pencils,
and, compliant, start our task.

Easy to answer most. We rate accommodation,
transport, our tour guide, without a problem.
Booking arrangements, seating at the play,
the guided tours – all this is simple stuff.

But then some questions on the play.
Harder here. No difficulty in evaluating
the performance and the staging.
But its appeal to us? How does one rate that?

I look around the bus. Some quickly finished,
reading, sleeping. Others serious, intent,
considering responses.

Not hard to estimate our mohawked friend's!
The half a play he saw quite clearly lacked appeal.
And judging by his hung over appearance,
he found alternative enjoyment. Expect
a *'Waste of time'* response from him.

On his own, as always, down the back
is Stephen, winner of that science prize.
Hard to read. I've talked to almost everyone
about their reasons to come here. By now
it's obvious that I'm professionally interested,
but Stephen is unwilling to be drawn.
Private. Remote.
Unsociable, to say the least.

What would he say?

They want to know about the play's appeal.
Intrusive. I'm not sure why I'm bothering
to fill this in at all. As far as tours go,
I imagine everything is satisfactory.

But do they really think
that I will bare my soul
and talk about that moment in the play
when Judas throws the silver to the floor
and weeping, finds the rope, to put
around his neck?

Too late to make amends.
too late for reparation. I understood
that feeling all too well. Too late

when Willy Meister died. Too easy
to accept the honours that were his.

But does this need to haunt me
all my life? There was a moment when
the dying thief turned to the central figure,
tried to patch together all his wretched life.

Can be done. There's still time if I choose
to use it. So even if I stay the outsider,
fringe dweller in humanity,
the guilt won't weigh me down.

The bus is passing Ettal,
and the Abbey looms,
its domed façade impressive in the morning light.
We look up from our dutiful attention to the form,
a brief distraction from the task.
Then faces turn,
intent once more,
to what they write.

    'Consolidation of my faith!'

That's all I've written
on their questionnaire.
Brief. To the point.
No one could quibble with that.
And that's the line that I will take
when facing scrutiny. It makes it clear
that I will be well-suited to my coming role –
leader of our church. The pang
of self-doubt that I felt that moment
when Christ spoke of the Pharisees
as whited sepulchres
should not be dwelt upon.

Conviction, firmness,
that's what the church needs
in this doubting age.
So when I am elected
the world will see how Bishop Justin
can fulfil the role.

Not like that hangdog figure of a priest
who's sitting opposite.
I've heard his story.
That's no way to be a model to the masses.

'It gave me hope.'

I can write this now.
Two days ago I saw no chance of hope.

I look across to where the other's writing.
I see him casting sideways glances at me.
They all do.
Everybody knows me as
a priest who's left the church.
A doubting Thomas?
No. It's not that God's not there.

But just that he's not here. With me.

But somehow, for the first time in this
dark night of the soul, I now feel less alone.
That moment at the end,
when from the cross,
there came that cry of agony, of desolation,
it gave me comfort.
If God's own son
could feel his father had abandoned him,
experience this pain, perhaps
there may still be a hope for me.

'*A very interesting experience!*'

Material of usefulness for the new series
of my show. TV evangelism needs
new blood, new stories, new experiences
to keep the viewers hooked.

If ratings fall,
a show is doomed.
We wouldn't want that, would we!

But these few days will give me
lots to talk about. So much that I can turn
to good advantage. And after all,
if Jesus could use parables
to get his message over, you must admit
there's precedent for what I do.

'*Poignant, yet comforting.*'

So poignant to remember that first time
when Rose and I came here to Oberammergau.
Once more to live those days, and see us
as we were, young doctor and his wife.
Blot out the intervening years, obliterate
the picture of the woman she is now.

Forgive me, Rose, for understanding
others' needs, but never yours.
Let me recall, and learn again
to love the Rose whom I will see,
for I will see her,
no matter how it hurts,
when I return.

The tour bus lurches to a stop.
Writers look up,
some irritated at the interruption.

Relief for others.
Coffee break.

It's just a small *Gasthaus*, white painted,
chalet style, festooned with splashes
of bright colour, pink geraniums that spill
from wooden window boxes. Inside,
the smell of brewing coffee comforts us,
a compensation for the early start.
Around the tables with the *streusel Kuchen*
we gather in small knots.
Fragmented conversations.

'Finished your homework?' laughs the Bull –
the name he told us all the football world
had known him by. Proud of it, clearly.
Some of them seemed to recognise the name.
He joins the older guy, the wannabee
Lothario. The one who'd eyed off every woman
in the group before Day One was over.
He views the Bull with some distaste,
but listens.

'Dunno about "appeal" – couldn't think
of anything, myself. Don't go for stuff like this.
Religious history, I guess you'd say.
What did you put?'

The older guy – 'Just call me Nate!' – his line
to all the women – looks a bit uncomfortable.

'Not sure yet what I'll put.
Haven't done that part.
There were bits of the show that got to me,
I'd have to say. Made me think
about a few things I'd forgotten.'

The Bull just laughs. 'Don't want to think too much.
The past's the past. Water under the bridge,
they always say. Cake's good, but.'

He wanders off. I watch old Nate
take hesitating steps to where the priest
stands solitary by the window.
Hear him say:
'A minute, father?
Got a question that
I'd sort of like to put to you.
Something in the play that got me thinking . . .'

They make their way apart. I hear no more.

'Finished yours?' The voice is Tommo Barnes.

We'd talked together over dinner,
one of the few I'd found prepared
for frank discussion of the reasons
he's come here. Nice guy.
It made me wonder
what, without the time in Vietnam,
his life might have turned out to be.
I smile.

'Fulfilled your obligation?'

He'd told me how this trip
was carrying out a promise.
'All OK?'

He hesitates, nods soberly.

'Perhaps old Jogger knew more than I realised.
Something about this place, this play . . .
Never been one for religion.
Told you that.

But watching all that yesterday ...
can see why Jogger found some peace
in working round his church.
Was thinking I might ask
if I could take his place.
Not going soft on all that God stuff.
But just the same
I've got some peace from this.'

'Something in that, Tommo,' comes another voice.

Joe Schmitke, who had told me
all about his farm the bank was now reclaiming.
'I reckon that's exactly what I put
for that last question on the form.
Appeal? Yeah, that was it.
It gave me peace.'

I think back to his story of the night he'd sat,
rifle on the table, his despair,
his sense of failure. Now a new serenity.
Feel envious. And say so.

'Yeah, sometimes things that look worst
aren't that way.
Sometimes good comes
from what looks real real bad.
My old dad always used to say
how God moves in mysterious ways.
I think it's helped me see that,
being here.'

'Didn't work for all of us, old chap.'
Tom Gilooley has been standing near,
and listening.

'If anything, it's been
the opposite for me. '

He gives no explanation, but I watch him
standing by the window, gazing over
rolling fields of green, grazing cattle
in this picture postcard countryside.

'Mind company?' I ask, and stand
beside him. 'You said, 'the opposite'?'

The silence lingers on,
against the hum of conversation,
clink of coffee cups behind.

'I guess I'd say it's been unsettling.
Made me take a long hard look
at things I've done.
Easy to be a Pilate,
wash your hands.
But dirt sticks harder than I'd thought.
Maybe it's time
to look again at what I'm doing.
But then maybe I'll get back home,
and everything will be just as before.
Who knows?'

I am surprised that such a careful man
will be so candid with me.

'Life's full of choices, Tom.
We've all got some to make.
Good luck with yours.'

The guide is calling. 'Time to return, please.
The driver says that we must go.'

But, as we go, I think of my glib words.

'Life's full of choices.'
Yes, for me also.

Last stages.
In the bus there is a sense
of ending.

In front of my seat sit the pair,
heads bent together,
conversation earnest.
The company director –
his name is mud, for sure –
no doubt about the numbers he's ripped off
if newspapers can be believed …
A question, that, but
this time things are pretty clear.
He gave me little explanation
for his presence on this tour.
'I'm simply filling in for Svetla's brother;
She had a ticket spare. Asked me instead.'

A bland convincing answer. Told me nothing.

Now they sit, long pauses in their quiet talk.

You see now why we come, each ten years
to this place?

A gesture of contrition?

We know our family is guilty. We need to do
whatever lies within our power.

So that explains the home for derelicts?
Your way of life?

It's little, but it's our attempt at reparation.
And you?

I'll need to think about it.
I won't deny that there are things
I also need to pay for.
To compensate.
But what you ask,
that I should come and work with you –
that needs more thought.
Don't shake your head.
I mean it. I will think what I can do.

Not money, Jiri.
That is not enough.
We need to give ourselves.
So many lives were lost.
Or ruined.

Not just by them.
I am my father's son.

Low voices murmur on.
But soon we will be there.

Irmgard moves purposefully down the aisle,
collecting forms. Wise woman.
If her little flock disperses, there'll be
slim chance of gathering these.

The five are still together,
hand their sheets to her
with half-shamed laughter.
'Not really a tour of the sort we're used to.
Don't take it personally, what we wrote.
You've done a good job, love.'

But only Len looks up and smiles.
'I got a lot from being here.'

Mick raises eyes to heaven,
smiles sarcastically.
'Well, mate, it was your trip.
Glad it worked for you.'

She pauses by the teacher,
a man one would have thought
well used to forms and record-keeping.
He shrugs, and indicates
he's not yet finished.
It would be interesting to know
what this tour's meant for him.

Across this morning's breakfast table,
I'd asked him whether he was going back
to yet another school.
He shook his head.
'Thinking of a change of life.
May move into the other end –
aged care could be a good direction for me.
This trip has given me a chance
to think about some things.'

What things?

Across the aisle, brisk and efficient,
our lady CEO hands in her form,
with compliments to Irmgard .
'You do a very good job of administration.
Not easy, with a group of such diversity.
The offices in Oberammergau
run everything so well.'

It must be fellow-feeling.
I'd imagine that she runs her show
with just the same control.

She's been at pains to make quite clear
her role is business management.
'Not the religious side;
that's for the churchmen.
It's their field.'

I've listened to her querying
the costs and structures of this Passion Play,
watched her evaluate expenses,
estimate the numbers and the likely profits.
But wonder.
How did she feel about the play itself?
A business model only, I suspect.

Suddenly we're into city streets,
and into Munich. So it's over.

'A final drink before we part?
A chance to say goodbye
before we go our separate ways?'
It's Francis, always in the role of host,
so from the bus we wander back into the bar
and make pretences that we'll keep in touch.
No one is fooled.

But as the group disperses, separate ways,
Alicia is beside me, shrewd and knowing.
'Well, my dear.
Did you get what you wanted?'

I am embarrassed, but I laugh.
'Was I too obvious?'

'No, very skilful, on the whole. A little nosy,
just at times. But then, I knew what
you were up to. So what is next for you?'

Ah, that's the question. I answer honestly.
'I don't know yet. I have the flight home
for some careful thinking.'

'Think carefully indeed, my dear. Whenever
I've let heart rule head, I've rued it later.'

'So now? What are your plans?
Have you made any changes?'

She laughs, a little wryly.

'I won't pretend I've had a lightbulb moment.
No sudden drama on Damascus roads.
But this has been a chance to pause.
And think.
Take stock. Evaluate.
We've done a lot of talking in this time.
Francis and I will do quite well together.
He's told me things … I understand
much better where he's coming from.

And, best of all, he likes me as I am.
No need to play a role, put on facades.
I can relax, just be myself.
You've no idea how much relief this is.'

We're silent for a time, both lost in thought.

'But I must go. Francis is waiting.'

We smile companionably.
A shared 'Good luck!'
Then she is gone.
It's time for me also.
Time too to think and make decisions.

Caroline – Changi Airport

How that word sums it up.
I am in transit.

Around me all the buzz of airport lounge.
The crowds of travellers,
arrivals weary as they trudge
to baggage claims,
then out into the humid dark
of Singapore, its tropic night,
its frangipani air.

Eager anticipation of departure,
for those who start their journey,
bright-eyed and forward looking,
waiting boarding calls.

Or those, like me, suspended in this transit point.

I know where I have been.
But what my destination?

The lives I've entered, in these days –
the ones who've given me a key,
allowed me in,
the others who have left me
just with clues for speculation –

I've entered other worlds,
shared others' lives.
Who was it said:
'I am a part of all that I have met'?
Small wonder that I'm not the person
who, naïve, departed,
worried only whether I'd return to him
or find myself discarded.

Cara mia – his private name for me.

I listened to his voice this morning,
wondered . . . even as I ached with love,
if this is so?
Am I indeed his Caroline?

He wants me back, that's clear.

'But would you leave her for me?'

His silence was the answer.

I think of them, these people,
and their stories.

Decisions made, and choices.
Guilt that burdens lives.
Betrayals that remain to haunt them;

betrayals haunt us all.

But any transit time must come to ending.
Directions must be chosen.

Some destinations ask too high a price.

I think again of Kaspar Schisler's words,
the prayer he might have made
as he looked out upon destruction of his village,
the deaths at Oberammergau.
His work.

I must accept the truth, the truth I have denied.
I knew full well what I was doing
when I came back.
It was my choice to come.

No more.

In spite of all my scepticism,
my doubts, uncertainties,
this journey has brought changes.
I laughed at the idea of pilgrimage.
So glib.

I am indeed a part
of all those I have met,
and must learn who I am.

Endings are beginnings.
So while I cannot see what lies ahead,
my journey too must end
as I return from Oberammergau.

Acknowledgements

This book has been the product of many years of writing, and even more decades of thought. Over this time I have been indebted to many people for their interest and support.

I owe special thanks both to my late husband, Noel Volk, who first listened to me talk about the idea over thirty years ago, and always wanted to see it written, and to my partner, David Harris, who has continued to spur me on with love and faith whenever my confidence faltered.

Many thanks also to my daughter, Felicity Volk, a truly fine writer, who has been constantly interested, encouraging and properly critical of this book. I could not have wished for a more astute and generous writing partner.

My Senior English students over decades of teaching have reinforced my belief that Chaucer's *Canterbury Tales* is both one of the greatest works of western literature and also a magnificent tapestry of life.

Finally, my heartfelt thanks to all those who have read sections of the work, drafts along the way, or who have provided information about various aspects of the tales. Each of you has had such special input that alphabetical listing is the only possibility.

Jude Aquilina

Claire Bell

Peter Bishop

Karl Cameron-Jackson

Bruce Dawe

Alison Hastie

Anne Jantzen

Geoff Page

John Pfitzner

Tony Schick

Nick Volk

Chris Wallace-Crabbe

Keith Welzel

Mark Worthing

To all at Wakefield Press, especially my publisher, Michael Bollen who, from the moment I outlined the concept, said 'We'd be interested in that!' No writer can ask for more!

Wakefield Press is an independent publishing and
distribution company based in Adelaide, South Australia.
We love good stories and publish beautiful books.
To see our full range of books, please visit our website at
wakefieldpress.com.au
where all titles are available for purchase.
To keep up with our latest releases, news and events,
subscribe to our monthly newsletter.

Find us!

Facebook: facebook.com/wakefield.press
Twitter: twitter.com/wakefieldpress
Instagram: instagram.com/wakefieldpress